Soul Discovery

(Soul series book 5)

Miranda Shanklin

Soul Discovery

By Miranda Shanklin

This novel is a work of fiction. Any resemblance to actual persons, living or deceased is coincidental. The characters, names, plots, or incidents within are the product of the author's imagination. References to actual events or locations are included to give the fiction a sense of reality.

Copyright 2016, Miranda Shanklin

All rights reserved. No part of this may be reproduced, stored, or transmitted in any form, by any means without written consent from Miranda Shanklin.

Cover design, Paper & Sage Designs 2015.

ISBN: (Trade Paperback): 978-1546390077
  (E-book)

DEDICATION

As always, I have to dedicate this book to my husband and my kids. They get just as excited as I do when I finish a book and it is finally ready to publish. They watch my white board to see how much progress I am making and do their best to not distract me when I am writing.

Other books by Miranda Shanklin

Soul Journey
Soul Series Book 1

Soul Redemption
Soul Series Book 2

Soul Knowledge
Soul Series Book 3

Soul Freedom
Soul Series Book 4

Soul Discovery
Soul Series Book 5

Coming soon:

Guardians of the Origin trilogy

Miranda Shanklin

ACKNOWLEDGMENTS

I have so many people that have helped me get to where I am today. My parents have always instilled in me the belief that I can do anything I put my mind to. They have always supported me in everything that I have tried and encouraged me and even given me a hard push when it was needed. I can't ever express how much their love and support has helped to shape me into the person that I am and given me the confidence to chase my dreams.

My husband and children have sacrificed so that I can chase this dream. I am unbelievably blessed that they have picked up the slack and taken care of the house and our animals while I have been lost in my own world writing. They have supported me and encouraged me as I embarked on this new journey.

My friend Ari, who has been amazing in helping me by spending hours on end reviewing, correcting, and giving advice. I could not have gotten through this book without her.

My beta readers who read this book as fast as they could and still gave me feedback on typos and sentences that just didn't work right. I was able to continue this process because as soon as they were done they were asking when I would be getting the next book to them.

The people that have bought my book and couldn't wait for the next one to come out make the work all worth it. I love to hear about how you feel about my books. If there is something that you loved or something that you thought just didn't feel right is always good for me to know. I thank all of you who take the time and hopefully get some enjoyment out of my books.

CHAPTER 1

I am really nervous about today. We finally have all the arrangements made and all the requests organized. Today is the first day we are allowing magickal beings from other realms to come and experience our realm. There are a few from each realm that are already here but that was not by their choice or ours. Every once in a while, the Origin would open a passageway and bring someone from another realm here to our realm. We don't know why they were brought here or even who they are but they have managed to integrate themselves and not be discovered. The only reason we know about it is because we are connected to the Origin.

The information the Origin gives to us is limited to what it wants us to know. We are the Guardians of the Origin so we have certain information we need in order to do that job correctly. What I can't figure out is why we need to know about the magickal beings that are already here. That must be important to something that is going to happen if we are given that knowledge.

At breakfast, I look at the others and see they are just as nervous as I am. It makes me feel better they feel the same way. I don't want to be the one that is paranoid while everyone else is fine with it.

Rayne rolls her eyes. "Sitting around here obsessing about what could go wrong and what the faeries and trolls are up to is not going to help. We need to roll with it and see what happens."

As much as I love that Rayne speaks her mind I can feel she is as nervous as the rest of us. That speech was just as much for her as it was for us. I have to admit she is right though.

We finish our breakfast and take the portal to the Origin. As soon as we step through, I can feel the familiar calming effects of the wooded area where all magick originated from. While we have to be careful to not let anyone else figure that out it is always helpful that it has a calming effect on us. We can draw on that power if we need it and will be able to handle any situation that presents itself.

We open the passageways and let the Guardians of the passageways in each realm know we will be ready in a few minutes. We open the portals and get everything ready for the first arrivals.

It has taken us quite a while to determine what order to bring the other realms in. We are trying to keep the faeries and trolls from being too close but none of the other realms trust or even like the faeries. It is a delicate system that has the potential to go very wrong very quickly.

I take a deep breath and let it out slowly to calm myself more. "We can't put it off any longer. We might as well get this started. I'm sure the other Guardians are getting a little upset with having to deal with the impatient people scheduled to come through today."

The others nod and we turn to the passageway to the elfin realm. They are by far the nicest and the ones I like the most. We decided to let them come through first and get to where they wanted to go. They would be out of the way and not have to deal with any of the other realms.

I smile when Zenia the Head Guardian of the

Passageways in the elfin realm comes through. I really like her. "Hi, Zenia, it's good to see you again."

She grins. "Thank you for letting us come through first and getting out of the way. It is generous of you to accommodate us like this."

"We know how much you want to keep to yourselves and the only reason you want to come here is to learn about another realm so we are happy to help you in any way we can. We hope you all enjoy your time here in our realm."

She laughs. "I'm sure we will find it interesting and will learn a lot. I don't mean to offend you, but I doubt many of our elves will want to stay longer than their current tour is scheduled. They will miss being able to connect with the land and the magick."

I smile. "You aren't going to offend us. Our realm is very different from yours and I can see where your elves would like to come and learn but not stay too long. I can't say the same for our witches though. I think there might be quite a few that would rather stay in your realm where they are able to feel the magick and live where they don't have to hide who and what they are."

"I am surprised to not see any witches here to come to our realm. I thought there would be quite a few of your witches here that wanted to explore the other realms."

"We actually told them that tomorrow is the day they can begin to tour the other realms. We thought for the beginning day it would be too much to keep track of for the comings and goings. We decided today would be arrivals and tomorrow would be departures. After that it will not be as many all at once and we will be able to do them both any given day."

"That sounds like a good plan. I admit I have it all written down and on a schedule but I didn't pay that close of attention to the dates."

"I know the feeling. I will be glad when this initial transfer is done. It will be a lot easier to keep track of once we have just a few on any given day instead of this influx all in one day."

"We are ready on our side if you are ready here."

"Yep, go ahead and send your elves through and we will get them on their way."

She steps back through the passageway and I can hear her giving the elves coming through a last-minute lecture on how they behave while in our realm and if they want to keep the privilege of traveling to other realms, they better not embarrass their kind by misbehaving.

I look at the others and can see them smiling. It takes some of the pressure off of us to know we don't have anything to worry about with the elves.

I greet the elves that come through the passageway. They all have a look of relief on their faces as they step through and see they are in the woods. I have to swallow the laugh that is fighting to come out.

I watch them and wait until I have their attention. "We want to prepare you for what you will experience here in our realm. While you have come through into a forest, you will find that is not the case for most of our realm. There are areas that are protected and remain untouched. However, the majority of our realm has been altered. You will find you will not be able to connect with the magick as easily and you probably won't be able to connect with the land at all. We don't want you to think something is wrong with you. It is just that all that has been done here in this realm has made it very difficult for either of those things. If you have any problems or want to go back to your realm early let your host know and they will contact us so we will be here to get you back to your realm."

The elves look at each other and I can see how nervous they are. I feel a little sorry for them. They are going to be the ones that have the hardest time adjusting. Everything they do works with the land and the magick. It will be hard for them to see how much our realm has taken advantage of and damaged our land here. I am sure some of them will stay their whole time just to learn what they can but I am also certain some of them will not be able to handle it and will want to go back early.

Penelope leads them to the portal they will be using and explains where they are going and who will be there to greet them. We have set up bed-and-breakfast locations for all the tours and the host at each location is a witch. It will make it easier if they have somewhere they can use their magick without being discovered. That way if they have any incidents where it just doesn't enter their mind to not use magick it is likely going to be where they are staying and not in front of a mortal. That is our biggest problem. Making sure the magickal beings that are used to using magick all the time don't expose their magick in front of mortals is a very tricky endeavor. Hopefully, we will be able to keep it from happening but I am sure we must get at least one or two out of mental institutions.

When Penelope has finished explaining it all to them she leads them through the portal. She returns a few minutes later with a smile on her face. "The host is very friendly and is making them feel more comfortable and going over the different things in that area."

I smile and turn to the portal for the goblins. They are next on the list. I am really hoping we can find a way to get rid of the odor in their realm. They have tried everything they can find and nothing has worked. We made sure the first place they are going to is set up with extra clothes that they can shower and change into. We also made sure there are extra washers and dryers so the clothes they bring with them can be washed to get the smell out. We want them to enjoy their stay and that isn't going to happen if everyone moves away from them to get away from the smell.

Greta the Head Guardian of the Passageways in the goblin realm comes through and smiles. "I wanted to make sure you are ready before I send our group through."

We smile at her and I respond. "Yep, we are running on time and are ready for your goblins to come through."

She nods and steps back through the passageway. We can

hear her giving instructions and then we see the group of goblins come through. They all kind of huddle together like they are afraid something will attack them.

I smile at them. "Penelope is going to take you to your host in a minute I want to let you know what will happen when you get there. First, we have it set up for you all to take showers and we have clothes waiting for each of you. While you are showering and getting changed, your clothes you brought will be washed and dried. We want you to enjoy your time here so we are removing the smell from your realm from your clothes. That way you will be able to move about in our realm without people shying away from you."

They grin and one says, "We thank you for thinking ahead and helping us. We were afraid we would be exiled due to the smell from our realm. It is nice to have a host that is considerate and helpful."

I smile and Penelope leads them to the portal they will be using. She gives a few last-minute instructions about what to expect on the other side of the portal and then leads them through.

She comes back through shortly after and we laugh at the look on her face. She scowls. "I would like to see all of you be that close to them before they showered. I know you said the smell was bad Annisa, but I couldn't imagine living with that. We really need to find something that will get rid of that smell."

Rayne looks distracted. "I have a theory on that but it will have to wait until this all settles down. I think I know what is causing it and how to fix it."

We snap our heads over to her shocked but don't have time to say anything as Heath the Head Guardian of the Passageways in the troll realm steps through.

He looks around to see if anyone is there with us. "I wanted to make sure you were prepared for my trolls to come through."

I smile at him. "Yes, we are ready, go ahead and send them through."

He disappears through the passageway. Instead of last minute instructions all he says to the trolls before he sends them through is "Remember what I said."

I glance around uneasily at the others as the trolls come through the passageway. Trolls are big so I have to look up when talking to them. I smile even though I am nervous about setting them loose in our realm. "Keep in mind you are bigger than most in our realm. People will notice you due to your size. Therefore, when you are away from your shelter make sure you are not using magick and you follow the rules that your host gives you. She is not trying to control what you do but is trying to make sure you stay safe while in this realm. She will give you the information you need to not get noticed as much and not attract attention of the authorities."

They watch me with expressionless faces. I sigh and indicate to Penelope to take them through the portal. She also gives last minute instructions before she leads them through and they give her the same look they had given me.

When she returns, she has a concerned expression on her face. "They seemed excited once we stepped through the portal. They went from serious to excited in a matter of seconds. It was weird."

I sigh. "Just wait the worst is coming next."

CHAPTER 2

The moment I have been dreading is fast approaching. It is now the faeries turn to come through. I know the faeries and trolls are up to something but I can't figure out what it is yet. They want to look for something in our realm but I have no idea what it could be. The only thing I can figure is they know the Origin is here somewhere but don't know where or even what it will be. I am glad they can't sense it since they are entering our realm on the Origin.

Drake the Guardian of the Passageways in the faerie realm comes through the passageway. He smirks at us. "It is time for the faeries to come through are you ready?"

I hate the condescending tone he uses, but it is not worth saying anything. If we try to stay on good terms with them, it will be easier to keep an eye on them. "Yes, we are ready. Go ahead and send them through."

He disappears, and he doesn't say anything to the faeries before they step through the passageway. I look at the others and can tell they don't like that anymore than I do. It seems the faeries have been given their instructions before the passageway opened so we wouldn't overhear them.

The group that comes through immediately looks around

trying not to miss anything in their surroundings. I'm not sure if that is because they want to make sure they know their surroundings or they are already looking for something. It is hard to tell if it is general curiosity or if they have an agenda. I decide it doesn't really matter since their reasons won't change anything.

"Welcome to our realm. We want to make sure you are safe and you enjoy your time here so please listen to your host when you arrive. She will give you the instructions you need to blend in while you are in that area. Also, please remember you can't use magick or let anyone know about your magick away from your shelter. The doctors here will lock you up thinking you are crazy if you tell someone you are a faerie and have magick."

They look surprised. The one standing in front responds "Your realm does not use magick like ours does but that doesn't mean we are incapable of performing tasks without it."

I smile. "I didn't mean to imply you didn't. I wanted to remind you it is not something that is used here. I understand it is natural for you to use your magick and wanted to make sure you remember it is not what is done here."

Before things can get any more awkward Penelope leads them to the portal, she will be taking them through. She gives a few last-minute instructions and then lead them through the portal.

Landon was fine all the other times she had led a group to their destination but this time he watches the portal intently until she comes back through. I see the look of relief on his face when she comes back within a couple of minutes. It looks like none of us trust the faeries.

The rest of the day goes smoothly. We greet and escort each of the groups to their destination. I am glad when we are done and able to go back home. It is more exhausting than I thought it would be.

When we get home, we all flop on couches in the living room. Chase mumbles, "I didn't think it would be so tiring to stand in the woods all day."

Rayne laughs. "If all we were doing was standing in the woods, it wouldn't have been tiring. We were controlling the passageways all day. Didn't you feel the magick you were using to open only the one we wanted open and making sure the others stayed closed until it was time for them?"

He thinks about it for a minute. "I didn't realize that was what was going on. It felt so natural I didn't even realize that we were doing it. We need to figure out a way to do this without draining our energy. We are all so worn out that if something were to come after us now we wouldn't be ready."

Landon interrupts, "After today it won't be that bad. The problem today was they were all trying to open their passageways to our realm, and we were working against them to keep them closed until we were ready for them. We won't have that anymore. Now we will have a definite schedule on when the portals are to be opened so we won't have to fight them like that. I think they were all so excited they wanted to open their passageways so they could listen while we brought others here. They all knew it would be going on all day here. Now they don't know when each realm will have access to ours so they won't all be trying to listen in."

"What about tomorrow? We will open all the passageways tomorrow to let the witches go to the other realms. Won't that be just as difficult?"

"No because it will be the other realms in control of the passageways. We control the passageways into our realms. That way the Guardians in each realm can decide to not let someone or anyone from any realm from crossing into their realm."

"That makes sense. I'm glad we don't have to control them all."

I laugh as the others look around trying to figure out what is causing the sound that sounds like someone is knocking on the house, not just the door.

I look around at their confused faces and giggle. "Come on in dad." Now they all turn to me completely confused.

My dad and the other adults all appear in the living room. My dad is grinning and my mom is rolling her eyes at him.

I look around and can tell that the others are putting it all together. "Apparently, dad thought it would be funny to knock before they came in."

They laugh. Then dad jumps right into business. "So, how did it go today? Any problems?"

I sigh and Penelope answers him. "It all seemed to go smoothly. I was a little concerned about the trolls but don't have anything concrete. They were all serious and didn't say anything when they first passed through but as soon as I took them to their destination they got really excited. The faeries acted exactly like we thought they would but everything else went smoothly. I think the others just want to explore but the faeries and trolls are definitely up to something."

Ethan interrupts. "They are looking for something but I don't think it's the Origin. I think there is something they think is hidden in this realm because they were denied access for so long. I think they have also figured out that some of them along with the other realms have been taken to this realm. We still need to figure out why that happened. We know the Origin had to have had a reason to do it but we don't know what that reason could be."

Landon's dad Derek interjects. "We have been trying to figure that out ourselves. We don't know any more than you do on why the Origin brought magickal beings from other realms here. We don't even have any theories because we don't know where they came through or even what they have been doing since being brought here."

Landon adds, "Whoever it was, they integrated into our world and not be discovered. I know some of them have been found, and that is where all the fairy tales have come from but there are more who were not discovered. It also makes me wonder if they have married and there are now children or adults that are half mortal and half magickal being. We could run into a whole new being. If there are hybrids out there they will be something that nobody has ever seen before. We don't know what they could be capable of. That is most likely what the faeries and trolls are looking for. They probably want to find those hybrids and use them. No being is going to not pass their heritage down to their children. They would have had to teach them how to use their magick and not be discovered. We have no idea what could result from a pairing with a mortal."

We sit there and let that sink in. None of us had thought about that before. Now that Landon has brought it up it is something that sounds very reasonable. Now we have to figure out what to do about it.

Chase voices his opinion. "I think that is the best theory. We need to keep an eye on who the faeries and trolls interact with. It would make sense they would want the freedom to travel about so they can find as many of them as they can. They could easily pass one hybrid off as someone they want to take back to their realm so they can be together. They could be trying to get all the hybrids to their realms so they can train them and recruit them to their cause."

Rayne huffs out a breath. "Great so now we have to babysit and make sure they are not trying to hijack the hybrids. With how the contract is written we can't stop them from going to the faerie realm if they want to go. We are going to have to come up with some creative interview questions to figure out if the person going really wants to go or if they are being forced to act like it. We also need it to look like that is not what we are doing. We don't want the faeries and trolls to know we have figured out what they are doing."

I ask, "How do we know the hybrids are something they would be interested in? We have nothing to indicate they are more powerful or anything like that. For all we know their magick could be diluted because of the mortal blood. Just because our magick is in our souls doesn't mean that is the case with all beings. I think the magick is passed on in the other realms. So, wouldn't it make more sense to be looking for hybrids with other magickal beings instead of with mortals?"

Penelope brings up the other option. "We also don't know if the magick is passed to the mortal offspring will be so much more powerful because it won't have anything to fight against it. All mortals have the ability to tune into the magick but most don't realize it. Therefore, the magickal being can enhance their magick by combining their bloodlines. They could be more powerful than anything we have seen yet. I think that is what the faeries and the trolls are counting on. I think the whole diluting the blood line the Faerie King threw out there was just to throw you off. He didn't want you to know what they were really looking for when they came here. If they made it sound like they didn't think the offspring would be worth anything we never would have considered that was what they were looking for. The biggest question is why do they want them? There has to be something they planned that would make it where they needed the hybrids."

Ethan adds, "I think they are still trying to find a way to take over the other realms. They think if they have the hybrids then they will have the needed power to overcome the other rulers and take over the other realms. The rulers have been able to fight against the Faerie King but if he has the power of the hybrids, then he thinks he will finally be able to beat them all. It will tip the scales where they are not all equal in power but he will have more power than them."

I sigh. "So, we now not only have to protect our realm but the others too? Like our job was not hard enough, now we have to take care of everybody else."

Mom laughs. "Honey that is what happens when you are the most powerful. We already know the Faerie King would not win against us because of you and the Origin but the other realms don't have that. It is up to you to use the power you have to protect those that are not able to protect themselves. It may be a lot to take on but not more than you can handle. It may seem overwhelming right now but you will be fine."

I nod my head to show I understand what she is saying. I'm still not sure we will be able to do this but know we have to try. I am hoping we will have enough power to overcome what is headed our way.

CHAPTER 3

Everything seems to be going well. We haven't had any complaints from anyone and the hosts are checking in every day and all the visitors are doing well. They are not having any problems with the trolls or the faeries so we are relaxing a little. We also are not getting any notifications from the other realms that there are any problems with any of the witches that have traveled there.

We have set up a few things in the woods to make it more comfortable while we are here during the day to monitor the passageways. We bring in a table so we can play card games and have chairs so we don't have to sit on the ground. We bring books with us too so we can continue our education on magickal beings while we are here.

It is quiet and we don't have much going on today so I look at Rayne and ask, "What is your theory about the smell in the goblin realm? We really haven't talked about it until now."

She looks up. "I think it is from a spell. When the Faerie King started showing his hand and trying to take over the other realms the other rulers did what they thought was best to protect their realms. Of course, this is from so long ago that nobody really knows anymore what was done. It has been passed down to each Faerie King that they are to continue to take over the other realms and the other rulers have been taught how to protect and expect what the Faerie King will do. I think when it all started and the ruler in the goblin realm did a protection spell it resulted in the smell. I doubt that was her intention, but that is what the result was. The reason they can't get rid of it with magick is because it would remove the protection she cast."

I think about what she said it makes sense. "I wonder if we can provide a different protection spell and then be able to dissolve her spell to get rid of the smell. I know we won't be able to take hers down until there is something stronger in place but if we put one up, then her magick should recognize it is no longer needed."

Penelope joins the conversation. "Do you think we will be able to break a spell that is that old and powerful? It has to be extremely powerful to affect the whole realm and to hold out all time."

"I think if we all do it then it will work. We will need to be connected and combine our power to be able to pull it off."

Just as I say this the adults appear in the clearing. Mom smiles. "It's about time you figured it out. We couldn't tell you what needed to be done you had to figure it out. We will keep an eye on things here while you guys go to the goblin realm and take care of that."

We walk over to the passageway to the goblin realm. It opens a few minutes later and we step through to find a confused Greta. "Is there a problem?"

I smile. "No there isn't a problem but we do need to speak with Queen Genevieve. Is she available?"

Greta nods her head and leads us to the Queen's house. When we get there, the Queen greets us with a smile. "What a pleasant surprise. I have been informed there is no problem but you wish to speak with me."

I smile and introduce the others to her. "There isn't a

problem but we think we may have found a solution to the problem of the smell in this realm." She raises her eyebrows in question but waits for me to continue.

When I am done telling her our theory she sits quietly for a couple of minutes to think about what we have told her. We give her the time she needs to come to a decision.

She lifts her head and looks at us. "I am grateful that you have taken the time to try and help us. I do have one concern though. If I allow you to try what you are proposing what is it you will want in return?"

I look at her shocked. "We don't want anything in return. We simply want to help you. It is horrible you have to live in such conditions and we are only trying to help."

It is her turn to be shocked. "You truly do not want payment for this service?"

I shake my head. She looks at us with a new respect. "I will allow you to attempt this spell. I also will give you a payment for your services. I will pledge our allegiance to you. We will be your allies and if you ever need our help in any battle or with any problem, you will always have the support of the goblins."

"That is very kind of you but it really is unnecessary. We truly just want to help and I don't feel comfortable with you pledging your allegiance to us."

She waives her hand in dismissal. "All I am saying is that we will be your allies. We will still have the same relationship we do now but if you ever need aide, we will be there to lend you whatever aide you need."

I smile. "We accept. It is always nice to have allies."

We walk outside and I see that Rayne is doing her best to not show how disgusted she is with the smell in the realm. I have a hard time not laughing at her face as she tries to keep it neutral.

Queen Genevieve is not able to hold her laughter in. She looks at Rayne as she laughs. "It is really not insulting to us that you find the smell here repulsive. We find it repulsive as well but have learned to deal with it. I am actually impressed that none of you vomited when you entered our realm. That is the reaction most have when they are first exposed to it. Now that you have brought this theory I can understand why the magick would have gone this way. The best way to protect our realm is make it to where nobody wanted to stay here."

The Queen steps to the side so we can all stand in a circle and concentrate. We join hands so it is easier to combine our power. We concentrate and bring forth a protection spell that is very powerful. When we are done, we all take a deep breath and start concentrating again to bring down the spell that is causing the smell.

It takes us longer than I thought it would and takes more power than I had anticipated to first cast our protection spell, and then bring down the prior one. When we are finished, we are really tired.

The Queen is practically jumping up and down with excitement. I smile when I realize we are all taking full breaths instead of the shallow ones we had been taking before. The smell is gone. Well not completely gone, it is still clinging to the objects but it would only take a good cleaning and the smell would be erased from the goblin realm.

We smile at the Queen. She offers her gratitude. "I can't ever repay you for the service you have done for us. I am truly grateful for your assistance in this. We will always be your allies and you can depend on us for help anytime you need it."

"It really is a pleasure for us to be able to help you. We couldn't sit back and let this continue if there was a way for us to stop it. I'm really glad we could help."

Just as I am finishing a group of goblins approach very excited. We watch as the Queen gives instructions on what she wants done to wash the smell away from the items it is clinging to. In a few days there will be no trace of the smell anymore.

When she is done giving her instructions, she thanks us again and Greta walks back to the passageways with us.

We are about to leave when Greta stops us. "You are the first who have ever taken the time to try to help us. The others thought since it wasn't in their realm, they didn't need to do anything to help. We truly are in your debt. We are honorable and loyal so now that the Queen has publicly acknowledged we are your allies you will have the assistance of any and all goblins any time you need it. She didn't do that just as payment but as a sign of respect for what you were willing to do for us."

"We are honored to have you as allies. We were happy to help without such a commitment but we will gladly accept your offer. I only wish we had known sooner and could have helped many years ago. It's really a shame all the realms don't try and work together and help each other. Hopefully, we will be able to bring the realms together once we figure out how to neutralize the Faerie King."

She smiles. "We have all been trying to do that for centuries. It is not as easy as it sounds. He is stubborn and ambitious. He will not give up his quest to rule us all."

"We are more stubborn than him and we won't allow that to happen."

We cross back into our own realm. My mom wrinkles her nose at us. "Hopefully that will be the last time anyone has to endure that smell. Go get showers and throw your clothes in the washer. We will stay until you get back."

I stick my tongue out at her as we pass her to take the portal back to the house. We return to the woods when we are done. When we get back, we explain exactly what happened while we were in the goblin realm.

Derek raises his eyebrows in surprise. "That is a really big deal. Most magickal beings don't swear their allegiance to anyone. They will help another realm if it will not harm them or if it somehow benefits them but most of them keep to themselves and don't bother themselves with the problems from other realms. The fact that she was willing to do this even before you were successful says a lot. She has shown that she trusts us and will stand up for something. The goblins have always kept to themselves due to their small size and the smell. They have been left alone but now that will change. Every ruler knows the faeries and trolls are up to something so for her to say she will help knowing there will be a problem shows she has a lot of respect for you.

I was thinking we wouldn't call on them to help but you make it sound like we would be insulting them to not ask for their help. I thought it was just a gesture not that she really expected us to call on them.

Derek laughs. "You showed her you thought them equals by helping them. Most races have written them off, but you stepped up and helped them without expecting anything in return. Yes, you would insult them by not asking for their help. If you truly thought them to be equals, then you will ask for their assistance but if you thought them unable to handle the situation, then it shows you were only trying to win their favor by helping them."

I groan. "This is going to get really complicated really fast. Now not only do I have to worry about what the faeries and trolls are up to but I also have to worry about offending the goblins and try to get all the realms to get along with each other."

"Nobody ever said being powerful, and the leader was easy."

I roll my eyes at him and the adults go back to whatever it is they do all day.

CHAPTER 4

I am starting to wonder if we have been wrong about the faeries and the trolls. So far, they haven't done anything to raise our suspicion. They have been acting exactly the way everyone else is. They come for their tour, ask questions, interact with the hosts and the mortals and stay on their schedule. They move on to the next location with no complaints and learn about each area.

When I bring it up to the others, they don't see it the same way. They are more suspicious than ever. Chase practically growls, "They are trying to get us to let our guard down. They think if they stay on their best behavior and do what they are supposed to then we will stop watching them so closely."

Ethan shakes his head. "That's possible but I think they are just observing and taking notes right now. They must decide where they need to start. I think they have been sending scouts through so far. That way they can sit down with all the scouts have learned and decide from there what to do next. They will go off the notes and what they are learning from each location to figure out where the best place is to start their search."

Penelope adds, "That makes sense. They are acting like they want to learn about the locations because they actually do. The only difference is the reason they want to learn. The others all just want to explore a new realm while they are scoping it out to make a plan to get what they want."

Rayne sounds bored. "I think you're all right. Yes, they are sending scouts to figure out the next plan, but they are also trying to get us to stop watching them so close at the same time learning about our realm. They need the information and I think they sent faeries that genuinely want to learn about our realm. If they are really interested, then they will take in more about it. If they sent faeries that focused on what they are looking for then they miss some important factors about each location. That's why we aren't having any problems, the faeries that are here really want to learn and have a great interest in our realm."

Landon interrupts, "I think we need to back off and let them think we trust them. If they think we aren't watching them as closely they are more likely to move forward with the next step in their plan. We know there are all kinds of magickal beings here you have to know how to look for them. We will notice when they behave in a way that indicates they are looking for the other beings."

I try to get my point across. "Just because we have decided to not go looking for the magickal creatures or the hybrids doesn't mean they won't. We may want them to be able to live out their lives in peace but the faeries and the trolls want to use them to get what they want. We might want to start to track some of them down and warn them about what is coming. If they have integrated themselves, then they are most likely part of the witch world and know about the realms being opened. Most of the magickal beings will be in that category but the magickal creatures won't. They will have secluded themselves to somewhere they won't be discovered or bothered. Those are the ones we are going to have to find. If we can find them before them then they will be prepared when they are approached."

Penelope counters, "The problem with that is we don't have any idea of where to look and even if we did we can't go running off all over the globe looking for them and leaving the passageways unprotected."

I look around at the rest of them and am afraid of how they will react to my next suggestion. I take a deep breath. "I think Chase and I should be the ones that go in search of the magickal creatures while you all stay here and protect the Origin and monitor the passageways."

I expect them to be angry but instead they think about what I said. I am surprised when Landon responds, "I think that is the best solution. You have the power to be able to sense them and they will sense your power so they won't run and hide from you. You will also need Chase there to help watch for danger. While you are focused on tracking them down and talking he can be watch for any signs of a trap or ambush. You have to remember there is a chance the faeries and trolls could get to them before you and will wait for you to show up."

I look around at the others and am shocked to see they all feel the same way. Rayne laughs at the look on my face. "You thought we were all going to throw a fit about you going to travel the world looking for magickal creatures while we were stuck here monitoring the passageways, didn't you?"

I nod my head and she continues.

"It shows how much you trust us and how much faith you have in us you didn't even think twice about leaving the Origin and the passageways in our care. You automatically went with us being able to handle it all here while you guys are gone."

I am still shocked. "Why wouldn't I think you guys could handle things here? You are probably more capable of doing it than I would be."

Penelope giggles. "You are the leader and the one with the most power. You have a way of wanting to do everything yourself. We usually have to talk you into letting us help. You try so hard to protect us all even when we don't need it. The fact that it didn't even cross your mind we might need protecting shows how much you have come to trust us and our abilities."

Chase smiles. "And it's nice to see that you have finally accepted that I can go with you on things like this and not get hurt."

I roll my eyes. "I'm not that bad."

They all laugh but I can't get upset about it because I realize they are right. I will really have to work on that. I don't want them to think I don't trust them or I doubt their abilities I always want to make sure they are safe. I guess I should start letting that go and trust they can keep themselves safe.

We call our parents down and explain to them what we have discussed. They agree that Chase and I going in search of the magickal creatures is the best plan.

I look around when it is decided that this is going to be our plan of action. "Now we have the biggest problem to deal with. We have no idea what magickal creatures are out there or where to look for them. Obviously, the Thunderbirds and phoenixes will be our first stop but they already know a little about what is going on. After that we don't know."

Mom looks at us. "It's time you start looking some of this stuff up. It is always good to know what is out there. All you need to do is look up what is possible and where they would most likely be and then go from there."

I nod my head and we head back to the house and settle in with books to research what it is we will be looking for.

It takes a couple of days before we feel we have enough information to get started. I'm sure we are going to find some new information as we talk to the creatures so I don't think it is necessary for us to know about every creature before we start. We will always be able to come back and do more research if we end up coming to a dead end.

We sit down and start to discuss where we will go first and where we need to look.

I look around worried. "There are so many that we will

not be able to track them all down. There are also some I don't want to track down. Some of them are better off not knowing what is going on. I don't think the faeries or the trolls would be stupid enough to approach some of them."

Chase nods his head. "I think some of these are better left alone. Let them stay in their little section of the world doing what they do. There is still a long list of others we really should find. Some of them it will just be to let them know and not ask for anything. Some of them we are going to have to ask that they don't team up with the faeries and trolls. I don't think we should ask any of them to join with us. I don't want to do the same thing that they are. We don't need to recruit these creatures—we want them to be able to live out their lives in whatever way they see fit."

Landon agrees. "I don't think we really need them to join us. I think just letting them stay where they are without us bothering them is the best option. I do believe they need to hear the whole story about what is going on so they can be prepared when the faeries and trolls show up or to disprove any lies they have told if they get there first."

Rayne looks at Chase and I with worry in her eyes. "You have to remember each time you approach any creature it is possible the faeries or the trolls have gotten there first. You have to be on the watch to make sure you are not attacked before you even get to say anything. They could have been told you are coming to attack them so they would wait for you and will attack first."

I nod my head. I have already thought about that but haven't come up with a solution to that little problem yet. Fortunately, Ethan has.

"If that happens you need to just put a protection bubble around you both and wait it out. You have enough power to protect yourselves until they realize you are not fighting back. When they see you are only protecting yourselves, it will give them a reason to listen to you. If you try to stop them or come at them in any way, it will only reinforce whatever lies they have been told."

Landon adds, "Some of these creatures are going to be very hard to get into contact with. They will feel your power so it will be possible to find them but they won't be happy to be interacting with you. Most of them just want to go about their lives without being noticed. The fact that you are tracking them down and calling them out into the open is not something they will like."

I nod my head. "Yeah, I can see the notes where some of them will avoid contact with humans at all costs. At least if it will be hard for us to reach them then it will be the faeries and the trolls too."

Chase sighs. "Now we have to figure out where to start and how we are going to get there. If we are flying all over the world we will be suffering from the worse case of jet lag ever. We will also be gone for months that way. I hate to have our parents have to go with us so they can create portals whenever we are ready to move on to the next spot."

I smile. "I don't think that will be necessary." They whip their heads around to me confused and then my mom walks into the room smiling.

"I am going to teach Annisa how to create portals. I would teach you all but she is the only one with enough power to do it on her own. For the rest of you, you would have to combine your power to do it and it would drain you pretty quickly. This way Annisa can create the portals you need without that side effect."

I look around afraid the others are going to be a little jealous that I can do this and they can't. What I see surprises me. They look relieved.

My confusion must show on my face because Rayne says, "At least one of us can do this. I am actually glad any screw ups in creating a portal will be from you and not me. I don't have to worry about sending us to the wrong place. I have to let you do the work and I can go shopping in Venice."

I roll my eyes at her. "This isn't so you can go shopping. This is only for use in our jobs."

She smirks. "Retail therapy is in the best interest of all of us."

Mom laughs. "You can use it for things like that as long as you don't abuse it. It is important for you to have some stress relief every once in a while. Just remember to be careful where you are opening a portal to. You don't want to appear in the middle of a crowd of people. That kind of thing will be noticed."

I spend the rest of the day with my mom teaching me how to create a portal and how to determine where it is going to open. The good thing is mortals can't see a portal. So, if I accidentally open one around a lot of people and as long as we don't walk through, they will never know.

CHAPTER 5

The next morning Chase and I pack up a couple of bags to take with us. We have to pack light and only take what will fit into a backpack. We don't know how often we will be able to find shelter or how long each location will take.

When we get downstairs, we discuss the plan one final time. I say, "I think going to the ones that are the easiest to find is the best plan. That is what they are going to have to do at first too. Hopefully, we can get to them before the faeries and trolls but I don't think we will be that lucky with them all. While we are gone, you guys need to keep trying to figure out a way for us to find the hybrids. There will be some that want to go no matter what we say and that's fine but I want to make sure they know everything before they make that decision."

Penelope reaches up and hugs me tightly. "Don't worry, we will be fine. We know how to take care of things here and if we really need you, we can let you know and it will only take you a few seconds to get here. I am more worried about you and what you could be walking into. Just remember if you need us open the connection and a portal to where you are and we will be there in seconds. Our connection does not have a distance restriction so no matter where you are in the world you can reach any of us by talking to us in our minds. With the connection and the ability to create portals we are never far away from each other."

I hug her fiercely and step back. I am afraid to talk because of the lump in my throat. I know if I try to talk I will start crying. I hug each of them and then grab Chase's hand.

We waive as we step through the portal I have created. I turn away from the portal when it closes, my breath catches in my chest. We have stepped out on the edge of the woodlands of Greece. It is the most beautiful sight I have ever seen. We stand there taking in the sight for a minute.

I look over at Chase. "I know we have a lot to accomplish but I think we should take a minute in each location to take in where we are. It would be a shame to go all over the world and not appreciate the beauty around us."

He nods his head and leans down to give me a kiss. He pulls back. "As much as I don't like you being in danger I love that we are taking this trip together."

I laugh and face the forest. "Now I have to find where in that forest the creatures we are looking for are. I think we are going to have to walk for quite a while before I even begin to sense them. They are going to be hidden deep in the forest to avoid being seen or discovered."

It doesn't take long for us to lose all sense of direction in the forest. I'm not sure if we are walking deeper into the forest or just walking in circles. I look around me and throw my hands in the air frustrated. "It's so dense in here I don't know which way to go. For all I know we have been walking in circles for hours. How are we supposed to find the Satyrs and the Sphinx if we can't figure out how to get to the heart of the forest?"

He laughs and points up ahead. I stop and stare. Apparently, we have been walking deeper into the forest the whole time because I can see the beautiful creature watching us and know we have found our first magickal creature.

The sphinx is about 100 yards ahead of us and is watching us intently. I am surprised when I see the foliage around her start to move and then something I am not expecting comes into view.

The sphinx has a smug look on her face as she registers my shock. She turns and walks away. After a few steps, she looks over her shoulder to make sure we are following her.

We follow her deeper into the forest until we come to what can only be their home. It is situated in between trees that make it impossible to sneak up on them and it looks like they have a very soft bed of leaves.

When they have settled themselves, the sphinx speaks. "I can see you did not expect to find us both here. Yes, I am supposed to be the Greek Sphinx, and he is supposed to be the Egyptian Sphinx. As we both have the body of a lion and the head of a human nobody ever puts it together that we are the two halves of a whole. Obviously one male and one female and being the only of our kind would make one think we belong together but for some reason the humans never think that through. They have their idea of what things should be and that is the end of it."

I have to bite the inside of my cheek to keep from laughing as the male sphinx rolls his eyes at her.

She scowls. "Just because I am not looking at you, Giza does not mean I do not know you are rolling your eyes at me."

He laughs. "I cannot get anything past you Theoi."

She ignores him and resumes talking to us. "I apologize but it irritates me that the humans make up such outlandish stories about us. Do I look like some monster that was sent here to terrorize a town? I obviously don't have wings. I may know the secrets of the universe but what good would that information do for anyone. All it would do is create a person who was obsessed with trying to change the outcome of any situation they didn't like."

Giza clears his throat. "My dear, they are not here to listen to your reasons for what you do."

She glares at him. "I know why they are here. I am the one who told you why they were coming."

He laughs. "It is difficult to live for so long with someone who knows what is going to happen and when. I find it best to just go with the flow and let her do things in her own way."

This time it is Theoi that rolls her eyes. "I am simply trying to explain that I am not the monster I have been portrayed to be. Now because you are here, I have some information that will help you on your quest. Please understand I will give you the information but am only able to tell you so much."

I nod my head. "I understand. We have had dealings with the Thunderbirds and they explained the way it works with telling the future."

She nods her head. "Good, you will need to remember that. It is good you came to us first. We will not take sides. We have always been and will always remain neutral in all matters. It is not in our nature to choose sides. Our involvement would unfairly influence the outcome. As I know what will happen when, it is an unfair advantage and will upset the balance. Remember the balance must always be kept intact."

I nod my head to show my understanding and she continues.

"You are going to meet with many different creatures. Some will be helpful and some will not. Some will willingly help you while others will adamantly refuse to help. There will also be some that do not want to get involved. It is only fair for you to allow each creature to decide on their own if they want to be involved and which side they wish to be on. Trying to force their help will only make matters worse for you."

"I would never force anyone to help us. I had not even planned on asking for help from any of them. I want to let them know what is going on so when the faeries or the trolls contact them they will have a good understanding of the situation."

"Ah, but in asking them to believe what you are telling them and not blindly go along with the faeries and the trolls is asking for help. You are asking them to do something that will benefit your cause and therefore are asking them to help you in that cause."

My jaw drops. "I didn't think about it like that, but I see what you are saying."

She smiles. "You must also realize that some will say they are willing to help you when they have no intention of ever doing so. You will bring the news of something some of them have been waiting centuries for. Not every creature is happy hiding and will welcome the chance to come back out into the open. Some don't want to be bothered so they will tell you what you want to hear to make you go away. The good thing about those is they will do the same to the ones that are working against you. Be careful who you trust and who you believe."

I nod my head and her attention shifts to Chase. "You are the truth bringer but your power of truth will not work on magickal creatures. We are all designed to be resistant to that kind of magick. While you are able to force the truth out of magickal beings, you will be unsuccessful in doing the same with magickal creatures."

I see the worry that flashes through Chase's eyes at this revelation. He doesn't like that he will not be able to use his power of truth to get the magickal creatures to tell us what they really plan to do.

With one last look of sympathy for him she returns her attention to me. "You know the creatures are not their main goal. It is smart to reach us before them but you will not reach them all first. Some of them are looking for the creatures while others are looking for the hybrids. The hybrids are the key."

I stop myself before I ask her what she means by that. I know she won't be able to give me any more information on that subject. She has paused to see if I will ask or not. When she realizes I have refrained from asking she smiles.

"I am impressed you could overcome your need for information and not ask me to expand on my statement. For that restraint, I will reward you with one more important piece of information. While the hybrids are not fully from this realm, most of them see this realm as their home. They have a loyalty to this realm and its people over that of their heritage. There are some that have resentment to the realms where their heritage originates for not being allowed to be a part of that realm. They feel abandoned and do not wish to help those realms."

I smile as I realize she is giving me the information I need to be able to bring the hybrids over to our side. If they already resent the other realms, then it will be easier to convince them they are being tricked.

She smiles as she sees the understanding take root. She was able to give me information that is extremely helpful without revealing anything that would cause us to change the outcome.

I bow my head slightly in a show of respect. "Thank you for all the assistance you have provided. I will remember what you have given to me and use it in the way you intend."

She nods and lays her head down. Giza smiles at us and then lays his head down next to her.

I know that is our cue to move on so we turn and walk away from them. I look over my shoulder and find them watching us with smiles on their faces. I am glad they will remain neutral because I would hate to have to come up against them.

Chase is not as optimistic as I am. "They said they will remain neutral which means they will give information to the faeries and trolls if they seek it too. What is to stop her from giving them the same information we have and then they can use it to convince the hybrids to go with them?"

I grin. "Because the faeries and trolls are too arrogant, they won't be able to stop themselves from demanding more information. They believe they are better than the creatures and they will expect them to give them exactly what they want. I was only given the extra information because I was able to take the gift offered and not ask for more. I wanted to know what she meant, but I knew she couldn't tell me so I didn't ask. Because I respected her limitations and her position, I was rewarded. They will not be so lucky. I will be surprised if they make it out of there unharmed. I have a feeling they are going to offend her and Giza will not take that kindly."

    Chase chuckles as he realizes I am right.

CHAPTER 6

We start walking again. We have been walking for a couple of hours and I am really starting to wonder how big this forest is. I suddenly feel the presence of magick. I stop and look around.

Chase raises his eyebrows in question but doesn't say anything. I whisper, "We are being watched. There are satyrs surrounding us."

He instantly tenses and starts studying the trees. I roll my eyes at him. "I promise we don't mean you any harm we just want to talk to you. I can feel your presence so please come out so we can talk to you."

They slowly start to emerge from the trees. It is weird to see men with legs like a goat and tails and ears of horses. I have to swallow my laughter as some of them stumble out of the trees. The one that seems to be the leader sighs heavily and looks at us.

"I am Sam the leader of the satyrs. I can feel the powerful magick you possess. Who are you and why have you entered our forest?"

I smile and try to be as pleasant as I can be to show them we have no intention of harming them. "My name is Annisa, and this is my husband Chase. We simply want to come and let you know what is going on and that you might be approached by either faeries or trolls."

He laughs. "Faeries and trolls have no access to this realm. They are only brought here slowly one by one and even that is rare."

"Now that the Guardians of the Passageways are present in this realm they now have access to our realm. The passageways have been opened. They are here and they are recruiting. They are trying to tip the scales in their favor so they can try and take over all the realms."

Sam laughs. "What makes you think we would have anything to do with any of that? We have no interest in getting involved in your problems."

I continue to smile. "We did not come here to convince you to join us. We simply want to let you know what is going on. We are fine with leaving you on your own to live your lives the way you want to. We have no desire to change your way of life."

He looks at me like he is studying me. "Why would you come all this way just to tell us we were going to be bothered by beings from another realm? There is nothing in it for you to come here and not ask for something in return."

"The only thing we ask in return is that you remember we came here and we do not wish for you to do anything for us and we have no intention of disrupting your way of life. We will not interfere with you enjoying the forest and your drinks and will only periodically come here just to check on you and make sure you don't need anything. I understand you have been surviving here for centuries without our assistance but we will help you if we can."

He continues to watch me as if he doesn't know what to think of what I said. When he realizes I will not say anything else his eyebrows shoot up into his hairline. "You truly are not going to ask for anything more?"

I shake my head and look at Chase. He also shakes his head and we wait to see what their reaction will be.

He studies us for another minute and then throws his arms in the air and smiles. "Come join us in celebrating our understanding."

"Um, can you please elaborate on what that understanding is?"

He laughs. "You will not bother us but will let us live out our lives as we see fit. We will not help the faeries and the trolls. We will continue to enjoy our lives here in the forest and once we turn the faeries and trolls away, we will be left alone."

I smile. "That sounds like a good understanding." He gestures for us to follow him and we don't want to offend him so we follow to where they are leading. I'm not sure how we are going to get out of there without drinking with them.

I look at Chase and can see the uneasiness in his eyes. He is just as worried as I am on how we will get out of this. It seems that most of the group is already drunk so they most likely won't notice if we don't drink the drinks they give us but the leader doesn't look like he is drunk and he is watching us with a smug smile.

We get to their village. I am pretty impressed with the set up. They have used things they found in the forest to create elaborate tree houses. I wonder how they ever got it finished if they drink all the time. I figure they must have done it when they first arrived and then began their unending drinking.

Chase and I look around impressed with the area they call home. The leader is still watching us as he leads us to what looks like a central area for them all to gather. We find seats and the leader brings us drinks. I can smell the alcohol as soon as he gets close to us with the cups. I'm not sure how I will do this without offending him. I smile and accept the cup. As soon as I have it in hand, I say, "Your homes are very impressive. I love how they integrate with the forest and feel so welcoming."

Chase smiles and asks, "How did you come up with the designs? I love the look of them."

We are hoping to distract him with conversation so he

won't notice we aren't drinking the drinks he has brought. He takes a long swig from his cup and responds. "When we first came to this forest, we spent a long time setting it all up. We had vowed to not drink until it was done and then we could make up for lost time after we had everything the way it should be. We have been making up for those years ever since. We now live our carefree lives and enjoy ourselves. We can mate every so often and our fauns are raised in the Roman countryside. We have the best of both worlds. We get to enjoy ourselves and still carry on our genes but not be bothered with the daunting task of raising the children. Once the fauns mature the males are sent here and the females stay and raise the rest of the fauns. We can then enjoy our time with our sons without the all the interference like other creatures have."

I ask, "Don't you ever wonder what you are missing while the fauns are being raised so far away? You are not there to help guide them to be the satyrs you want them to be."

He laughs. "The females know what they need to do to make sure the fauns know where their place is and how they are expected to behave. If any of the females were to try and change the way things are done, she would be removed from her position and would only be used for mating purposes. We are all happy with our way of life and have never had to remove any female, and no male has ever dishonored us with his behavior."

Chase looks at me to make sure I am not getting angry with his attitude. I have no right to get angry. This is how their culture is and it works for them. I have no interest in coming here and telling them they have to change their way of doing things when none of them have any desire to change. I smile at Chase to let him know I am fine with what is going on.

I then notice that Sam has been watching me closely for my reaction to what he has said. I smile at him. "I understand that your culture is very different from ours. Your way of doing things is the way you prefer things. I have no desire to come here and tell you I think you need to fix something that none of you feel is broken. I would not like to live in this culture but that doesn't mean it is wrong. It is just different than what I am used to. You are all happy with how things are so there is no need to change anything."

He nods his head and takes our cups. He laughs at the look on my face. "I knew you would not drink the drinks we brought, but I wanted to see how serious you were about not wanting us to change our way of life. I should probably tell you we do visit the fauns and help the females to raise them. I wanted to paint the worst possible picture to see how far you were willing to go. I appreciate that you are willing to let us continue our way of life even if it is not the way you believe it should be. Let me show you around the camp. I am pretty proud of the work we have done."

I am impressed with the work they have done. It is intricate work that creates the houses and buildings they have built. In order to integrate them into the trees it is very delicate work that would have taken a lot of concentration. I am thinking the part of his story where they had remained sober until the work was done was the truth. They would not have been able to do this delicate and intricate work while drunk.

After he has given us a tour and explains about the way things work in their village, we walk back to the central gathering place. He brings us cups of water and smiles at the relief on our faces.

He says, "I apologize for making you believe the worst about us. I had to see how sincere you were about the deal we were making. I really do appreciate you are not trying to come in here and change the way we do things. We have lived this way for centuries and our system works for us."

I smile. "I wouldn't want anyone to come to our place and demand we change so I refuse to do that to anyone else. If it was a system that left half the population in misery then I would want to help but from the way you explained the way it was done it seemed like everyone was fine with your system. I have no idea how it all works so I would have no right to come in here and tell you to change everything."

He smiles. "I suppose your next stop is with the fauns?"

I nod and he continues.

"I would like to go with you if you don't mind. The females there are very protective of the fauns and I would hate for one of you to get hurt when you show up unannounced. It has also been some time since I went and visited with my children. I was planning on going soon and this is a good reason to go earlier."

I smile. "It would be nice to have someone there to help smooth things over. I understand that some of our stops will be more dangerous than others. But I do have a question if you don't mind me asking."

He nods his head with amusement in his eyes. He knows what I will ask. I ask anyway. "Why do the grown males live so far away from the females and the fauns?"

He laughs. "I am surprised you took so long to ask and that you have not figured out the answer to that already. As I said, the females are very protective of the fauns and they do not like all the drinking and activities that occur here in our camp. They like to keep the fauns away from it all until they are old enough to understand. This was the solution we came up with. We are allowed to come for visits and our mates stay there. We are allowed to see our children and be part of their lives as long as we are sober when we arrive. We are also not allowed to drink while we are there. We don't stay long but we do go often. This way we do not lose our mates and are still allowed to visit our children even though we enjoy our drink."

I smile. "I'm glad you could come to a compromise that works for all of you. It would be really sad if your races died out because you could not come to an agreement."

I will show you to where you can stay tonight and we will be on our way first thing in the morning.

CHAPTER 7

I am surprised at how comfortable the bed is. It is made with leaves bound together with moss. It is soft and I snuggle in close to Chase and am asleep in moments.

The next morning Sam is waiting for us. I miss coffee already. It is only one day and I am already realizing this is going to be a difficult trip without coffee in the mornings.

He smiles and passes me a cup and I let out a contented breath when I smell the coffee. I turn to him with a confused look.

He laughs. "We may live in the woods but we make our way in to town every once in a while to get supplies. We have a standing order that is dropped off at a warehouse. We go in the middle of the night to pick them up when we will most likely not be seen."

I laugh. "I guess I pictured you living off the land and making do with what you had here. I never even considered you going into town for supplies."

We talk for a little bit while we have our coffee and then start on our journey. He looks over at me. "It is a long journey to where we are going I hope that is ok with you."

I smile and create a portal. "It is just a step away. I'm

sorry but we have many others to visit and we don't have time for all the travel so we are using portals to get from one to the next."

He grins. "I was hoping you had a quicker way to get about."

We step through the portal. I walk through first then Chase and Sam follows behind us. As soon as we step through, I stop dead in my tracks. I have a spear aimed at my throat. Chase freezes not sure what to do and Pan starts to laugh.

I am thinking we have walked into a trap when the spear is removed and the laughter is echoed. The faun who had been holding the spear inches from my throat looks to be close to reaching maturity. He smiles and gives Pan a hug. "Dad, we weren't expecting you for about another week."

He hugs his son back. "That was my original plan, but I was approached by these two and knew if they tried to reach your camp on their own they wouldn't make it past you."

Chase glares at him. "You could have warned us. I would rather be prepared if there is a chance someone will point a spear at my wife's throat."

"You are the one that let her go through the portal first. If you are that worried about it maybe you should go through first."

It is my turn to glare. I can tell by the look in Chase's eyes that he will be going through the portals first from now on. I sigh knowing there is no way to change his mind after what had just happened.

Sam claps Chase on the shoulder as he gestures to his son. "This is Seth." They lead us to the camp. It is the same as the one we have just left. The satyrs must have put this all together before they went to their camp and made their village.

We are getting guarded looks from everyone we pass. The children are all very curious but the females will not let them get close to us. I get the feeling the only reason we are being allowed to pass through at all is because of who we are with.

We reach the largest house and walk in. The boy shouts, "Mom, Dads here, and he brought visitors."

A beautiful woman makes her way into the room. Even with the legs of a goat she is still beautiful. She smiles, and it lights up her face. "Sam, it's so good to see you. I wasn't expecting you for another week."

He smiles and wraps her in a hug. "I know, Lique, I came early when I found out what has been going on. I have brought the people you need to talk to so we can make sure all the children remain safe here."

She looks over his shoulder and then says to her son, "Seth, you are to go back to your guard position. You should not have left. I know you are excited to see your father but it is not time for your shift to be over yet. Go back and relieve Sary until it is his turn."

He wants to say something but one look at the disapproving look on his father's face and he closes his mouth and leaves.

She turns to us. "If Sam has brought you here then I know it must be important. He would not accompany anyone to our camp without good reason. I am also glad to not see any signs of too much to drink last night in any of you. Please have a seat and I will bring some food for us all. I'm sure Sam only offered you coffee this morning and you must be starving."

We smile and sit down where she indicates. I offer to help her but she shoos me away so I sit with Chase and Sam and wait for her to return. It is only a few minutes later that she returns with the food. She is right I am starving. We have only eaten a few granola bars and things like that while we were hiking through the woods yesterday. We eat in silence.

When we are done eating, she looks at us expectantly. I can tell she is waiting for me to explain our reason for being here. I look at Chase and he nods his head slightly to let me know I should just get to the point.

I look back at her. "We are only trying to inform all the magickal creatures what is going on. We do not want anything from you and we do not want to change the way you conduct your lives. The passageways to the other realms have been opened now that the Guardians have been appointed for this realm. The faeries and the trolls are trying to recruit for their goal of taking control of all the realms. We are informing you that we have no intention of disturbing you or your way of life no matter what they try and tell you."

She looks to Sam, and he laughs. "I gave her the story we agreed on to test any magickal being. She didn't even flinch. When I said everyone was happy with our system, she smiled and said she had no intention of changing that."

I interrupt him. "I am an outsider looking in at your way of life. It is not the same as mine but that doesn't mean it's wrong. You have just as much right to live your life as you want to as we do."

She holds her hand up to stop me. "I see how the conversation went. I appreciate that you don't want to change the way that things are run, but have you thought about what the faeries and trolls will do to us to try and force us to join them? How can you be certain we will not come to harm even if we do not get involved?"

It is Sam who answers her. He must have known she would ask this question because he has an answer at the ready. "They will not come to your camp. As far as they know it is a camp of women and children. They will want our camp where all the men are. They want warriors not those they feel would be in the way. Just because we know you women are more ferocious than we are doesn't mean they will know that. We are also going to have our rotation upgraded so there are more of us men here at any given time. I know you don't like to have too many of us here at one time because we tend to get together and forget the agreement but until this situation is under control, we are going to have to have more here. I promise we will behave ourselves while here. I am also going to limit how much we drink so we can deal with them when they arrive. I believe all the men in camp will have no problem taking a furlough from the drinking in order to ensure your camp is secure and protected."

She smiles. "I accept your offer. I believe that is the best solution." She then looks over at me. "I appreciate you bringing this to our attention before they arrive. I know the only way Sam would have brought you here is if you had proven to him you were sincere and not trying to use us for something you wanted. Is there anything we can do to show our appreciation?"

I smile. "I only ask that you remember what happened while we were here. We don't want to have a strained relationship with any magickal beings or creatures. We are making our way to all that we can find to let them know our intentions before they are fed lies by the faeries and trolls. We don't want a conflict to happen simply because we didn't let anyone know of our intentions."

"I believe that is a smart move. You should be prepared that not all magickal creatures are going to be as accommodating as us. We are willing to listen to you and make our own decision. Some will attack first and ask questions later. They will see you showing up as a threat to them and they will fight to protect themselves first and then worry about who it is that just showed up."

"We know and we are prepared for that. We are hoping as long as we protect ourselves and not fight back they will realize that and stop to ask questions."

She laughs. "You are very optimistic, aren't you? I hope your plan works but I have a feeling you will find it harder than that."

Sam sighs. "Don't scare them dear. They are doing the right thing and trying to help everyone. I think they are prepared and are smart enough to accomplish their goals."

I see her eyes light up as a new idea occurs to her. "You spoke with the sphinx while you were in the forest. That is what led you there first. That was a very smart move. I hope you were smart and earned her favor. She is very kind to those she favors."

I grin. "Yes, that is what led us there first. I had some experience with someone that has knowledge of the future so I was practiced at not pushing for more information. She was very kind and very helpful to us."

She beams. "You must have worked with the Thunderbirds then. Beautiful creatures and they are put in such a bad spot. No matter how much they try to not be involved they always end up causing damage. If you have worked with them and earned the favor of the sphinx, then you should be fine on your journeys."

"Thank you. I appreciate your advice. We can use all the help we can get on this trip. We know it will be difficult and trying but it is also a necessity. We really need to let everyone know we don't want to force them to fight for us. We will welcome any help that is offered but we will not request it."

She raises her eyebrows. "You will not ask for assistance? That seems a little reckless. It would be better to ask and be turned down then to not know what help had been available if you had only asked."

"I understand what you are saying but this is our responsibility and we will not ask for anyone to put themselves in this position. If they would like to help, then they will offer, but I don't want anyone to think we are going on this trip to try and convince them to help us."

She nods her head. "I understand your thought on that and I hope you receive the assistance you need."

We leave them to discuss their next plan and we make our way out of their village. I don't want to create a portal in their village and wait until we are quite a ways away from it before I create one to our next location.

CHAPTER 8

After I create the portal Chase informs me of his intentions with his jaw jutting out stubbornly. "I will be going through first. I refuse to let you be in that position again. You can give me that little smirk all you want, but I am going through first."

I laugh and hold my hands up in surrender knowing I would not win if I fought him on this. Chase steps through the portal and gasps in surprise. I smile as I step through to join him.

He is looking around confused. I grab his hand and lead him down the beautiful beach just above the line where the ocean's waves are coming up on the sand.

I smile up at him. "We need more time to just enjoy life. We spend so much time trying to prevent the next tragedy or fix the one that just happened that we don't take enough time for us. I thought we could use a little break, so I brought us here to watch the beautiful sunset."

He let out a breath, visibly relaxes and pulls me close. He leans down and give me a tender kiss. He pulls back but not far as he rests his forehead against mine. "Baby, I would love nothing more than to have more of these special moments with you. Where are we by the way?"

I grin. "Does it matter?"

"You don't know do you?"

I giggle. "Actually, no I don't. I saw a picture of this beautiful beach and the amazing sunsets and I really wanted us to see it so here we are."

He chuckles. "It doesn't matter where we are as long as we are together it is perfect."

We sit on the sand and watch as Mother Nature paints the most beautiful sunset I have ever seen. When the sun has dipped below the ocean, we watch the stars start to emerge. We lay for hours pointing out the constellations and the groups of stars we think were the prettiest.

When I see a shooting star, I point it out to Chase. "Make a wish."

"Baby, I don't need to make a wish I already have everything I could possibly ever want."

I roll on my side propping my head on my arm so I can look at his face. "Have I told you lately how much I love you?"

He smirks. "No, I don't think you have."

I push against his chest to sit up and he grabs me around the waist to hold me there against him. "Baby, I was joking. I know you love me as much as I love you. You don't have to tell me in words all the time. I see it in the way you look at me, the way you take into consideration if I would like something before you wear it and in every move you make. You make me see how lucky I am to have you every day."

My eyes start to tear up as he is talking. He reaches up and brushes a tear from my cheek. "Don't cry, that's a good thing."

A grin forms through tears trickling down my face. "I'm not crying because I think it is bad, I am crying because that is the most romantic thing I have ever heard."

He kisses me softly and we settle back into the sand to look at the stars for a little while longer. When it starts to get a little chilly Chase finds some driftwood and makes a fire for us to sit next to. I don't want to leave this beach and the romantic interlude we have to our chaotic lives so we camp on the beach for the night and take a little more time for us.

The next morning, we know we have to get back to our agenda for the trip. We make sure the fire is completely out and packed up our stuff.

When I am putting my back pack on Chase reaches over and pulls me to him. "No matter how crazy our lives get we have to remember to have more nights like this. That is what makes it all worth fighting for."

I smile. "Sounds like a great idea to me. Now I don't mean to break our romantic moment but you can't go first through the portal this time."

He narrows his eyes at me.

"Hold on, let me explain. We are going to the Sirens next. Put earplugs in before you can go through and you won't be able to hear if there is any danger lurking."

He reluctantly nods his agreement as his body tenses and his hold on me tightens. "Fine, I can see your point but I want you to keep a hold of my hand. When you go through if there is a problem squeeze my hand and I will pull you back through. If you don't run into any problems tug on my hand and I will come through to you."

I look back at him over my shoulder before I step through the portal. I shake my head at the look on his face and the stiffness in his body. I'm glad he didn't fight me harder than he did about this.

I step through the portal and stopped just outside of it. It is utterly silent. Even the waves crashing against the rocks below are barely audible. I instantly get goose bumps all up and down my arms.

Chase doesn't wait for me to pull him through and steps out behind me. What happens next has me struggling to keep up. As soon as he steps through we are surrounded by women. Their appearance alternates between the most beautiful women I have ever seen and old hags all hunched over. I can hear a melody but it is faint and almost like white noise in the background.

As I look around I realize they are all focused on Chase and he is staring wide eyed around him. He must only be able to see the beautiful women and not the hags. I feel a pang of jealousy as he continues to look at the women around him seemingly forgetting about me.

I am not ready to deal with him finding other women attractive. I know he will but I don't have to like it. I glare at the women around us. "If you don't mind I would prefer you not seduce my husband with your siren song."

The women all laugh. Chase smiles and I scowl. Chase turns too. "Their laughter is the most beautiful sound I have ever heard. I think it's safe for me to take these earplugs out now. I would be much more helpful if I could take part in the conversation and not have everything barely reach me."

I shoot daggers with my eyes at him. "If you know what's good for you, you will leave those earplugs in until we are off of this island."

He furrows his brow confused about why I am upset. I turn my glare to the women surrounding us. "I came to talk to whoever is the leader of your group. I would prefer to not have to drag my husband through your village."

One woman steps forward. "I am Salina. I am the one with whom you wish to speak. You cannot bring a man to our island and not expect us to protect ourselves. We will always protect ourselves from men."

I sigh. "I understand that you feel all men are your enemy but my husband is with me because some of the places I need to travel he will need to watch and make sure I am not in danger."

She nods her head slightly and the eerie silence returns. Chase scowls at the change and I throw another glare at him over my shoulder before returning my attention to Salina. "I would like to discuss with you the visitors that have been allowed to enter this realm from the other realms."

Her appearance begins to morph back and forth between

the beautiful woman and the old hag once more. I am starting to understand that when they feel threatened, they have a hard time holding their shape. It seems I am the only one that can see the struggle.

She smirks at me when she realizes why I am staring at her open mouthed. "You can see the struggle in my form. You must be very powerful to be able to see through the glamour and see the hag form at all. I will listen to what you have to say."

I take a deep breath before jumping into the reason for our visit. "We have allowed the other realms to come through the passageways and visit our realm."

"Why would you do something like that?" she asks with a sneer.

"We thought it would be better to have them entering when and where we knew about it rather than having to track them down when they snuck through. The faeries and trolls are trying to recruit so they can have the power to take over all the realms. We simply want to give as many magickal creatures as we can advanced notice that they will try to elicit your help. We have no intention of coming here and forcing you to do anything you don't want to and we will leave your island and will not disturb you anymore after this meeting, but we wanted to let you know they are here. We thought it was only fair for all of you to know who has been allowed in our realm."

"So, you are going to the magickal creatures that couldn't possibly take care of themselves and not tell if visitors are lying to them? Let me guess, you will tell us exactly what you want us to do."

I take a breath. I can see this is not going to go as smoothly as I hoped. I just want to get the information out there and get Chase away from them. Salina is not going to let it be that easy.

"You say you don't want us to be forced into doing something we don't want. You are coming to my island and saying I am too weak to fight against the faeries and the trolls and they will force me into believing and doing what they want from us."

I glance over my shoulder at Chase for support. Unfortunately, his earplugs are preventing him from hearing our conversation. He is still watching the other sirens with fascination. I sigh and turned back to find Salina glaring at me.

"You don't get what you want right away and you look to a man to help you get it? I think it is you who might be too weak to fight against being forced into doing something that you don't want."

"I was only checking on him to make sure that your sirens had not succeeded in entrapping him. I did not mean to imply you are too weak to fight them. I wanted to give you a heads up that they were coming and they would be telling you lies about what our intentions are. We do not want you to change the way of your kind nor do we want you to leave your island. We will not interfere with you in any way."

She scoffs. "You say you don't want to interfere but you being here is you interfering. You want us to side with you and not help them so you are trying to get to us before they do. You are not different from them you are just trying to be nicer about it. I think we will make our own decision when the time comes. We will hear what they have to say and then we will decide who it is we will support."

I nod my head in defeat. I can tell I have insulted her by coming here with Chase and there is nothing I can say or do to fix that. If I had come alone, it might have gone better but to bring a man to their island is not something they were willing to overlook. All I can do is hope the faeries and the trolls make the same mistake or one even worse. I am really hoping they only send men and then Salina won't trust any of them at all.

In an attempt to leave gracefully I take one more chance. "Thank you for taking the time to speak with me. Of course, I will leave you to make whatever decision you feel is best for your sirens."

I turn and pull Chase back through the portal. I hadn't closed it when we stepped through so we are back on the beach.

CHAPTER 9

I whip around and glare at Chase. He shakes his head like he is clearing it from a fog.

He looks at me and his look turns too confusion. "Why are you giving me that look?"

"Oh, I don't know, maybe because you stood there and drooled over the sirens the whole time. You didn't even try and fight their song. You just stood there and stared at them and even wanted to take your earplugs out."

He reaches for me but I am still too angry so I step away from his hand. He sighs and looks at me with sad eyes and his shoulders slumped in defeat. "Baby, you know it wasn't me. It was that song. I had never heard anything like it before and it was telling me you were fine with me watching them. It made me think everything was fine, and they only wanted to entertain us."

I huff out a frustrated breath. I know I can't be too mad at him because it wasn't his fault.

This time when he reaches for me I let him pull me close. "I swear you are the only one I want. They forced a reaction out of me that was not natural. It always has been and it always will be only you for me."

I rest my head against his chest while he hugs me tightly. "I know, it hurt to see you looking at them like that. I know it was from their magick and you didn't really feel anything for them."

He chuckles. "I think I like it when you get jealous."

I scowl. "I wasn't jealous I just thought you should have fought against them more."

He starts to laugh. "Ok, baby, whatever you say."

I push away from him. "Alright, Casanova, time to go to the next place. I smirk at him as I create the portal.

He doesn't even give me a chance to say anything as he steps through the portal first. I roll my eyes and follow him. I am sure he is not going to give me the opportunity to go first again.

I step through and scowl. Chase is looking around at our surroundings trying to make sure nobody will attack us.

I can feel the presence of some strong magick but I don't see anyone around. I follow the feeling to a spot between some trees. I can feel it is concentrated here but I still can't see anyone.

I look up at Chase and smile. "I'm Annisa and this is Chase we are two of the Guardians of the Passageways here in this realm. We are only here to give you some information and will then be on our way."

Chase whips his head around as in the same spot that I had felt the magick a man appeared. Chase furrows his brow.

Standing there was the most gorgeous man I have ever seen. He stands about 6 feet and has the body of someone that keeps in great shape. His t-shirt clings to his body in all the right spots and his pants hang off his hips in the most perfect way.

Chase tenses and pulls me into his side. I giggle.

The man stands there watching us before he speaks. "What do the Guardians want with the dwarves?"

Chase looks down at me with a confused look on his face.

The man gives an impatient sigh. "Yes, I know that stupid

children's story led everyone to believe that dwarves are all about 2 feet tall and old men. Just because we are the guardians of the earth's minerals and precious metals doesn't mean we have to be able to fit in your pocket."

I laugh and Chase actually looks a little embarrassed. He then tightens his arm around my waist holding me to him.

I raise my eyebrows. "Who's jealous now?"

I wiggle my way out of his arms but he stays right behind me. I smile at the man standing there. "We don't want anything from you. We are here to give you information and then we will be on our way. Can you take us to whoever it is that is in charge?"

He nods his head and gestures for us to follow him. He leads us into a little village. It is beautiful with all the materials that they had used. Their houses and buildings sparkled and shined in the sun light. I can feel Chase tense and fight his instinct to pull me close and get out of here the farther into the village we get. I have to fight not to laugh. He doesn't like that everyone we pass could have been an underwear model for men's underwear. The men were the most gorgeous men I have ever seen.

All the way at the end of the village we come to the biggest and most beautiful cottage. Our guide knocks on the door and then opens it and leads us inside. Chase is right on my heels and not letting me get more than a couple of inches away from him. I chuckle as we are led to a sitting room.

We wait for about five minutes then the man that walks in makes me stare with pure shock. It almost hurts to look at him. He is perfect. Every feature you would think of as attractive on a man is accounted for. He has a woman trailing behind him but I am so distracted by the man's perfection I don't really pay her much attention.

She starts to laugh and I realize what had happened. I had spaced out while staring at him. She is too polite to call me out on it and apparently, she finds it amusing.

She smiles kindly at me. "I assure you that you are not the first and most certainly will not be the last to be captivated by

Drevin's appearance. I am Dani and my husband and I lead the dwarves."

She is average in appearance. Pretty but not beautiful, in my opinion, but that could be because we just came from the sirens.

Chase glares at me and then turns to Dani. "I apologize for any misconduct. We were just not expecting your appearance."

Drevin laughs. "Yes, most expect very small, old men with absurd names. That children's story has helped to conceal our existence, but it gives other magickal beings a false understanding of us. It is a double-edged sword."

I laugh. "I can see your point. However, your appearance has nothing to do with why we are here. We are here to give you some information and to prepare you for what might be coming your way."

Drevin and Dani sit back in their chairs and indicate for me to continue.

I take a deep breath and decide to just get to the point. Hoping this meeting will go better than the last. "We are two of the Guardians of the Passageways. Now that the passageways are guarded in our realm they have been opened to our realm. That means the other realms have access to come in and visit our realm and relocate here if they wish and meet the standards we have set. The problem we are facing is the faeries and the trolls are trying to recruit for their cause. They want to be able to take over all the realms and they are hoping to find the power and the beings here in our realm to make that possible. We are going to the magickal creatures and letting them know what is going on so they can be prepared for the visits. We also want to let you know we have absolutely no intention of trying to change your way of life or moving you from your home. We are not asking for anything from you except to listen to us and keep that in mind when you are visited by them."

Drevin furrows his brow. "If this is a problem, why are you allowing them access to our realm?"

"We have no proof that is what they are doing. So far, they have only sent scouts to our realm to determine where they need to begin to find what they are looking for. Until they make a move against us we have no cause to deny them access. We believe they are going to try and convince all magickal creatures we are planning to make them change their way of life and move from their homes to where we want them to do whatever it is we want from them. We have no intention of doing this. We don't see any reason why your lives should be disrupted or changed in any way. You have lived your lives for many generations with no problems so there is no reason to facilitate a change."

Drevin nods and looks at his wife. I can tell there is a silent conversation going on between them so Chase and I sit and wait patiently.

When they turn back to us, Dani looks sad and Drevin looks excited. Drevin is the one to respond. "We thank you for giving us this information. We have long ago retreated from human interaction as it only caused problems. We have a good life here in our village and are good at our job. However, there are times that things get a little boring and predictable. Dani prefers it that way as most of the women do but us men still wish for some excitement every once in a while. We will be waiting for your call when the time comes that you will need our assistance."

I look at him wide-eyed. "I didn't mean to imply that we are asking for your assistance. We simply wanted you to know we do not want to disrupt your lives or your homes."

He waives his hand in dismissal. "I know. You didn't imply that you were asking for anything. You came here to give us information. Now it is my turn to give you information. We will assist you in any way we can. The faeries and the trolls will come to us last if they come at all. They will think of us as we have always been portrayed. As they believe us to be very small and old men, they will not believe us to the warriors they are looking for. Now that you know we are very much in shape from our work with the earth you will have an advantage over them. We will go and meet some of the other dwarves and find their opinion on the matter."

He stands up and we follow him out of the cozy cottage. As we walk back through the village we are met with friendly smiles and waves. Drevin stops and talks to groups of people. He explains the situation and the wives get a resigned look about halfway through his story while their husbands get excited. It appears the wives all know that their husbands will jump at the chance for excitement. It doesn't seem to really bother the wives, just that they wished their husbands were not so eager for such excitement.

By the time we have made it through the village we know the whole village is in agreement that they will be helping us if we need it against the faeries and the trolls.

Chase has been quiet the whole time we have been here. He still has a brooding look on his face as we walked away from the small dwarf village. I make a decision I think will be nice for both of us.

I make the portal and Chase steps through first. He turns on me as soon as I step through. "Bringing us back to the beach does not change the fact that you sat there and drooled all over that guy back there."

I laugh. "Just like it didn't change the fact that you were ready to pull your earplugs out and waste away listening to the siren's song. I only brought us here because I thought it would be nice for us to come back here each night for some time away from all of this and a safe place to sleep. Since we don't know where we are it will be hard for anyone else to find us."

He sighs and then pulls me in and his lips crash into mine. His kiss starts out hungry, angry and possessive. It quickly calms down to breathtakingly sweet kiss. When he pulls away, he rests his forehead against mine. "I don't ever want to feel like that again. I hated watching you admire some other man. I'm sorry you had to see that with me and the sirens."

He then stands up straight and looks down at me

suspiciously. "You knew about the dwarf's appearance and took us there right after the sirens on purpose, didn't you?"

I smile innocently at him. He laughs as he realizes even though I won't admit it that is exactly what I had done.

CHAPTER 10

We watch another beautiful sunset as I snuggle in close to Chase and we watch the stars slowly appear in the night sky above us.

Chase leans over and kisses my temple. "I could stay right here with you forever."

I laugh. "Wouldn't you miss the others?"

"Yeah, but moments like this with you are far more important."

"But then moments like this wouldn't mean as much. If we had these all the time, then they wouldn't be special anymore. We are almost done. We only have three more places to visit and then we can go home and sleep in our comfy bed instead of the sandy beach."

"Just remember how to get us here so we can always come back and watch these amazing sunsets."

I sigh as I relax into him and drift off to sleep.

The next morning while we are packing up our stuff I can't help but think about how we haven't taken showers since all of this started and I am really starting to feel gross. I smile up at Chase as I walk down to the beach. My clothes are as gross as I am so I walk into the salty water fully clothed. I hadn't put my shoes back on yet but the rest of my clothes are going to at least get rinsed off like the rest of me.

Chase laughs. "You know with all the salt in that water you will not feel as clean as you think when you come out."

I grimace. "It can't be as bad as I was feeling after not showering for so long. Look at all the gross stuff coming out of my clothes."

He grins as he joins me in the water. He is still fully clothed as well. I wrinkle my nose as I watch the water rinse away the dirt that accumulated on us during our trip.

I feel a lot better as I step out of the water.

Chase smiles at me. "As much as I have loved having you to myself the last two nights, do you think we can get the last three done today so we can go home and take real showers?"

I laugh. "I was thinking the same thing. I don't see why we shouldn't be able to get them all done. None of the ones we have left should be too difficult. Since we are not going to the more aggressive creatures, it should make it a little easier. I wish we could go to the dragons and unicorns. I would love to see them in person."

"I know you would, but the dragons will take it as a personal insult if we just show up and the unicorns don't like to be disturbed. I think by leaving them alone we are showing them we don't want to change their way of life. By the time we are done news will have traveled that we have visited and what we have said. The others will know our position and will most likely think we didn't visit them out of respect."

"Or think we didn't think they were worth our time."

"I'm sure some of them will think that. If we show up then we are threatening and wanting them to pick a side and if we don't show up, then we don't think they are worth our time. Either way is not a winning situation for us. It is better to leave them alone and let them come to their own conclusions. Most of them will see our reasoning and appreciate it. The ones that don't we wouldn't have done any good visiting them, anyway."

"I know I just wish we could see them all. All these

creatures that I always thought were made up are actually real and it would be amazing to get to meet them all."

He laughs. "In time, my love, in time."

I create the next portal and gesture for him to go through. I have given up on trying to convince him to let me go first. I know it will never happen. As my clothes dry, they start to get a little stiff from all the salt in the water. I am ready to get this done and go home to a nice hot shower. Arguing over who goes first would be counterproductive.

When I step through my breath catches in my throat. The scene I am standing in is the exact replica of what I had imagined as a child when my mom would read stories to me. It is a magickal forest that has blooming flowers everywhere and tiny, glistening little pixies flying around. It is breathtaking.

Even Chase stops and stares in wonder. We are so caught up in the magick of the moment that we don't see the little pixie that is flying right for us. It is flying so fast that by the time I see it I don't have time to react before it collides with my forehead.

I instinctively put my hands up to catch the tiny creature before it falls to the ground. When I look down in my hand, I see a tiny little pixie. They look like a human with red hair, upturned nose, pointed ears and beautiful gossamer wings. She is not happy with me at the moment though.

She glares up at me and chastises me in her tiny little voice. "Don't you know any better than to just appear and then stand there right in someone's way? You could have moved you know."

"I'm sorry I didn't see you until it was too late for me to get out of your way."

"Well now that you have stopped me what do you want?"

I have to bite the inside of my cheek to keep from laughing. It is really cute to see this tiny little pixie so angry and try to look so intimidating.

I clear my throat. "I need to speak with your leader. We are two of the Guardians of the Passageways in this realm and we have some information for her."

The little pixie sighs. "I was hoping that was a rumor. Follow me. Hurry up and don't get lost. Make sure you are watching where you walk. I will not step in if you crush someone's house."

I look at Chase and can see he is having as hard of a time not laughing. We follow the pixie who is annoyed at having to slow down so we can keep up. We could have gone faster but we have to make sure we don't step on any toadstools and crush someone's home.

We make it to a clearing and she stops at a large tree. "Wait here."

She flies away before we can respond. I look at Chase and we are both doing everything we can not to laugh at the cute little creatures. We don't want to offend them but seeing her so angry and acting like she can do any damage at all to us is pretty funny. It is like watching a toddler trying to act like his lawyer father.

A couple of minutes later another pixie approaches us. This time the glimmer that is approaching is bigger and brighter than any we have seen yet. I watch with interest as we are approached. As she makes her way to us all the other pixies move out of her way and give a respectful distance for her.

I realize why we were brought to this tree as the new pixie lands on a branch that is eye level with me. I turn and smiled at the little pixie.

She stands tall and proud and I can tell she is trying to make her presence more significant. It must be hard being that small.

"I am Brooke. I have heard of your visits with others. So, it is true you have allowed the other realms access to our realm?"

I smile. "Yes, it is true. We had no reason to deny them access."

"You could have saved yourself all this trouble and effort trying to prevent an issue with the faeries and the trolls if you had denied them access."

"Yes, but I try not to punish others for the misdeeds of one. I believe giving you the information and letting you decide for yourself how you will proceed will be enough to keep them from being successful."

"You do realize they have already started to gain support?"

"No, I didn't know. I am sure the other Guardians at the passageways are aware of the situation. While we are on this trip they are taking care of things there. I will get a full report of all that has happened when I return tonight."

She raises her brow. "You are ending your trip to visit others so soon? You have not even visited half of the creatures of this realm."

I nod my head. "I know there are many more I would like to visit. However, we can only be gone for so long. We are hopeful that news will spread of our visits and other visits to other creatures will not be necessary. We are needed back at the passageways to help with the travelers."

"I agree. I believe that is where you are needed. We are aware of the situation and will not keep you from your duties."

With that she flies off. I look at Chase and he shrugs his shoulders. We find our way back to where we had come in at and I create another portal.

When I step through after Chase I am met with a scene I was not expecting. I look over at Chase. "I really wish our research had been based on the real thing instead of what was created to keep the creatures hidden."

He laughs. "I know what you mean. This is definitely not little men in green suits running around with pots full of gold."

I look around at the men with red hair that all looked like normal men. The one closest to us had overheard what Chase said and rolls his eyes at us.

We are approached by a laughing man. "I can tell by your expressions you didn't have the information about us that was up to date. We have had to adapt to fit in and not stand out in this world. You would never guess how hard it is to live in a world where everyone knows you cannot tell a lie."

Chase smirks. "But you also don't tell the whole truth."

He grins with mischief all over his face. "Very true but not everyone knows that. My name is Seamus. Yes, I know my parents thought they were hilarious giving me a traditional name and one that is associated with our kind since the beginning of time."

I open my mouth to respond but he doesn't give me a chance.

"I know who you two are of course. News of your visits has been traveling very quickly. I also know why you are here. Let me show you around a little and then we will talk business."

He walks around the little village and talks nonstop. I look over at Chase while our host chatters on and on about the area we are in. There is nothing significant in his chatter and I find my mind wandering. I am glad there will not be a test later as I don't listen to even half of what his is saying. Chase smothers a chuckle and follows along.

When we stop and Seamus pauses to take a breath Chase jumps at the opportunity to say something. "Seamus, I promise we will not ask you any questions. You don't have to keep talking to keep from giving us the opportunity to ask you anything."

He looks sheepish. "I wondered if you would catch on to that or just assume I like to talk."

Chase and I laugh. I look over at Seamus. "We really are just here to give you the information about the faeries and the trolls. We have no information we are seeking from you. Please relax."

He smiles. "I apologize. It is a defense mechanism that has been instilled in me since I could talk. If you don't give the other person the opportunity to ask a question, then you can't be forced to give information you don't want to."

"I understand and it really must be difficult for you."

"Not that much anymore. Now that our kind has faded away into legend it never occurs to anyone that is what we are. Since the legend is about little men in green suits, it helps that we actually look like normal people with red hair. It is only with people that know what we are I find myself falling back into that old habit."

"Well, since you already know who we are and why we are here, that makes things a lot easier. We wanted to come and make sure you didn't have any questions for us."

He gives a slight bow of his head in respect. "Thank you for finding a way to phrase that without asking any questions."

I smile.

He then looks at Chase. "They will use any trick they can think of. They are very sneaky and clever. You must keep an eye on them when they come through and check them when they leave. They will try to distract you with disruptions to sneak things back to their realm."

Chase smirks. "We already expected all of that and are prepared for it."

"Good, I'm glad to hear that."

CHAPTER 11

I grab Chase's hand and follow him through the portal to the last creatures on our list to be visited. I run into the back of him as he stops on the other side with no warning. He jumps to the side pulling me behind him while saying, "Damn, that hurt."

I look down and see little holes in his jeans with blood around the edges. I look to where we had come through to see what had caused them. I laugh when I see the trap that had been set. It is low enough that if you didn't know to look for it, you never would have seen it. Someone had sharpened twigs and placed them pointing up at a 45-degree angle so when you walked into them it would cut into your leg at your shin.

As Chase is examining his leg to see how bad the little cuts were I watch as we are surrounded by small stocky old men in brown robes resembling that of a monk. I am fascinated by the little creatures.

Chase is still cussing under his breath about the tears in his pants and the blood running down his leg.

I have to stifle another laugh as one of the old men grunts out in frustration "Don't be such a baby it is just a few scratches."

Chase glares at the gnome. I clear my throat. "We need to speak with your leader please."

The little gnome stands as tall as he can. "I am the one you are seeking. We have been expecting you. We set the trap in case it was not you that found us first. We know what the situation is, and are prepared to defend our land and treasures."

"I'm glad you have been informed of what is going on. Is there anything you need from us to assist you?"

He looks at me shocked. "You have the hardest job of all in this and you are asking if you can help us?"

I nod my head confused why he is so surprised.

He laughs. "We are the ones that need to be asking you if there is anything we can do to assist you. When the time comes that you need assistance we will be ready for your call. We have someone positioned to watch the portal at all times. All you have to do is open the portal and we will follow it to where you need us."

"I thank you for your offer and I will remember it if we are in need of assistance. We would be honored to have your help."

He smiles. "We may be old but there is still plenty of fight left in these old bones."

The rest of the group cheers.

I grin. "I'm sure there is. Thank you for your offer as well, and we will take you up on it if need arises."

He smiles back at me. "Now you can go back to your home and continue your work guarding the passageways. We will make sure the word is spread."

Chase finally loses his glare. "Thank you. We are anxious to get home. We want to see what all has transpired there since we have been gone."

We wave to the gnomes as we step through the portal back to our house. We have barely stepped through when Callie and Ghost launch themselves at us. I laugh as I catch Callie before she collides with my chest. Ghost has grown so much he knocks Chase over when he can't slow himself down fast enough. Chase and I laugh as he picks himself up off the ground and plays with Ghost for a minute. I carry Callie in my arms while I walk toward the house.

Chase is right behind me as we get to our room. I smile over my shoulder at him. "I am taking a shower in here first. If you can't wait, you are going to have to use another bathroom."

He laughs. "That's fine. I will use Penelope and Landon's shower."

I stay under the spray of hot water from the showerhead and let it relax my tense muscles. It feels wonderful to be taking a shower and washing off all the grime of our travels and the salt from my rinse in the ocean this morning.

When I get out of the shower I hear Chase laughing and Penelope yelling at him. I laugh and continue to put lotion on and get some clean clothes to put on. When I am done, I walk down the hall to see what Chase has done to annoy Penelope already.

I walk into their room and instantly start laughing. Penelope is still yelling at Chase who is ignoring her while he gets dressed with the bathroom door open slightly so he can hear her.

It is what she is saying that has me laughing. "If you are going to use my shower, you need to let me know first. How hard is it to open the connection and say 'Hey, Penelope, Annisa and I are back I'm gonna use your shower really quick'?"

As soon as I start to laugh Penelope spins on her heel and throws her arms around me in a fierce hug. "The only reason he is still alive is Landon came in here before I went in there. I would go in and grab something while Landon was in the shower but since it was Chase, I would have been very surprised if I had opened the door any further."

I am still laughing. "Sorry, I couldn't wait. I had to take a shower immediately when we got back. You can't imagine how gross you feel after going that long without a shower."

She wrinkles her nose and turns back to the slightly opened bathroom door. "You better hurry up and get out here and give your sister a hug especially after that little stunt you just pulled."

Chase comes out of the bathroom laughing and scoops her up. He swings her around while giving her a huge hug. "I missed you too, little sister."

She smiles and hugs him back just as tightly. I smile as their love for each other is apparent. They might bicker a lot but they are very close.

Landon walks in with Rayne and Ethan right behind him. "Is it safe to come back in yet?"

Chase laughs. "Cowards, you all waited out in the hall until she finished yelling at me."

Rayne smirks. "We're not stupid. She has been very grumpy since you two left and we were staying out of her way until she was done with her little tirade."

Penelope glares at Rayne. "I haven't been that bad."

Ethan laughs. "Even the trolls have been avoiding her."

She puts her hands on her hips. "They deserved that. They were being very arrogant and treating the goblins terribly. They didn't even take the time to realize the goblins don't smell bad anymore. They went right into the normal cruel statements the goblins have had to deal with forever."

Rayne rolls her eyes. "She has also taken to trying to make everyone treat the goblins better. She thinks it is her personal mission to make everyone treat them with respect."

"I don't see what the big deal is. They are being mistreated. Somebody needs to stand up for them. They have been pushed to the side and walked on since the beginning to time because of a spell that didn't go as they planned. It's not their fault and they shouldn't have to pay for it for the rest of eternity."

We all stop and stare at her in shock. Now that she has said that, we know exactly why she is so intent on helping the goblins, she can relate to what they are going through. She was the one that cast the spell that had ended with our punishment that we fought so hard to break free from. Now she saw the goblins being punished by a spell one of their ancestors had cast and she felt like it was unfair to them to have to continue to pay for one bad spell.

I walk over to her and hug her. "Ok, honey, we'll help them. We will make sure they start to get treated better."

When we pull apart, she glances around her. "We weren't expecting you back for at least a couple more days. What went wrong?"

I laugh. "Nothing went wrong. News was traveling fast about our visits and what we were doing. By the time we got to the last three they already knew what was going on and it didn't take us long at all. In fact, we did all three of them today."

Chase interrupts. "Can we finish this downstairs after I have had a chance to brush my teeth and feel back to myself again?"

Landon laughs. "Definitely, I was trying to find a nice way to tell you that you had horrible breath."

We laugh and Chase punches Landon on the arm as he walks by to go to our bathroom to brush his teeth.

When we are all downstairs, we tell the others about what happened at each of our stops. They all sit quietly and wait for us to tell them everything before any of them say anything.

When we are done, Rayne looks over at Ethan. "If the sirens side with the faeries and trolls and you come up against one of them, you better fight with all you have because I will not be so nice about you drooling over some hag that makes you think she is beautiful."

I laugh and Chase counters. "Oh, she wasn't nice about it either. Why do you think we went to the dwarves right after the sirens? She wanted to show me exactly how it felt to watch the one you love drool over someone else. Of course, I had no option, and it was all part of their magick while she was drooling over his looks."

I playfully swat him on the chest. "I was not drooling. I

was admiring. I'm married not dead and I am not the one that was ready to fall to her feet and waste away while she sang to me."

Rayne interrupts. "Seriously though, we are going to be in trouble if they convince the sirens to help them."

I smile. "I get the feeling the faeries and trolls don't put much faith in their women being able to carry out their instructions. I think they will take a group of men thinking they will be able to overpower the sirens since they are only bitter women. It will be the end of their recruitment if they take even one man so when they show up with a group of them I don't know how Salina will react. She was insulted I brought one with me and I would rely on him to protect me so if they show up with a group then she is likely to go into a rage."

Rayne smiles. "Good. I hope they don't make it back from that island."

Landon laughs. "Even if they went with all women, I don't think they could recruit the sirens. I don't see them leaving their island. They have a man free environment and won't risk going into a situation where they could face many men."

I look around at everyone. "I know you guys want to discuss all the possibilities and what we need to work on but I am ready to sink in to my comfy bed and get some sleep."

Penelope smiles. "Sorry, we didn't think about how tired you two must be. We can talk about all this tomorrow while we are at the passageways."

We say goodnight and head up to bed. I change into my pajamas and curl up to Chase. I am asleep before I even have a chance to tell him good night.

CHAPTER 12

The next morning, we wake up and it is really quiet in the house. I look over at the clock and jumped out of bed. Chase rolls over and grabs my wrist.

"Come back to bed. It's not time to get up yet."

I laugh. "It's 10:00 in the morning. It's past time to get up. I can't believe we slept so late. I wonder why nobody woke us up."

"Because they knew we needed some sleep. We have been on the go for the whole trip and we needed to get some good sleep in our own bed. Now come back here."

I crawl back into bed. He pulls me close with my back up against his front. He snuggles in closer to me and I relax again. I wake up about an hour later and nudge Chase and he grunts.

I laugh. "We need to get up or we won't be able to go to sleep tonight."

He groans as he rolls over onto his back. "Fine, but you should know I am doing this under protest."

"Duly noted, now get up."

We take showers and gathered up some food to take to the others for lunch. Then we step through the portal to meet with the others in the clearing. I can't help but laugh at the scene before me.

Penelope has her hands on her hips and is glaring at a troll that is trying to push a goblin out of his way with his foot. The goblin looks resigned to what is happening, and the troll is giving Penelope a challenging look.

When I laugh all eyes instantly dart to me. I stop laughing as they stare at me. Landon, Rayne, and Ethan have a look that says finally, Penelope has a look of anger and frustration I am glad is not directed at me, the goblin looks hopeful and the troll looks like he doesn't know how he should react to this new development.

The troll has stopped trying to push the goblin back and is no longer giving Penelope a challenging look. Penelope crosses her arms over her chest and gives the troll a smirk.

I sigh and look up at the troll. "We do not allow that kind of behavior here."

"How do you plan to stop me? I have every right to be sent through first. I am higher up than that stinky little thing."

I am instantly furious. I narrow my eyes, my body goes rigid and I take a fighter's stance. He takes a step back. "First, if you would get your head out of your ass you would realize the goblins don't stink anymore. We took care of the problem and have gotten rid of the smell. Second, you are not more important or better than anyone else. Everyone that comes here has the same status as a visitor. Third, I am the Leader of the Guardians in this realm and if you don't like my rules then you can go right back through that passageway and explain to your King why you are no longer allowed to visit this realm."

As I am talking I get closer and closer to him. What I don't realize is I am also rising up higher in the air so by the time I am done I am at his eye level and poking him in the chest.

As I calm down and come back down until my feet touch the ground again Penelope continues to give the troll a smirk.

When I am on the ground again she sneers, "I told you she wouldn't allow that kind of behavior."

I glare at the troll. "You were already informed this was one of my rules and I would not tolerate that kind of behavior and yet you continued to do it, anyway?"

He just stares back at me dumbfounded. He doesn't know what to say.

Chase looks at Landon and says, "We'll be back in a little bit."

He follows me as I march to the passageway to the troll realm. The troll continues to stand in the same spot unsure of what to do. As Chase passes him he gives the troll some useful advice. "You better come with us if you want to give your King your version of the story because that is where she is headed."

He instantly looks terrified but for once I don't care. I step through the passageway with no warning to the Guardians on the other side. Heath jumps up when he sees the look on my face and that Chase is right behind me followed by a troll with his head hung low.

Heath takes the scene in and then sighs. "Let me guess he thought that while you were gone, he didn't have to follow the rules and he didn't know you were back and got caught red handed."

I glare afraid of what will come out of my mouth if I start to speak. Chase nods his head. "I think we need to meet with King Sebastian."

Heath nods his head and gives his troll a sympathetic look.

We are led to the King and I instantly start in on him. "If your trolls do not learn how to treat others with respect or how to follow rules I will close the passageway from your realm to ours. It does not matter if I am there personally or if my Guardians are following my orders. The fact that he stopped his disrespectful behavior as soon as he saw me indicates he knew he should not be behaving in such a manner but decided to do it, anyway. Even after he had been told I would not tolerate such behavior he continued and challenged one of my Guardians. I will not permit this behavior to continue. You will either get your trolls under control or teach them how to behave in a civilized manner or you will not be allowed in my realm."

The King listens to me until I am done he then turns and glares at the troll we had brought back. He then looks back at me. "I can assure you this behavior will not be a problem. I will be putting a stop to it this instant. I apologize you had to come here and bring this to my attention. My trolls have been informed they are to behave respectfully to all while in your realm no matter the being. I will reinforce this idea personally."

"Thank you. I hope it doesn't become such an issue as to close our realms to each other."

While glaring at the troll whose head is hanging even lower than before he continues. "I can assure you that will not be the case. My trolls will behave in a way to not bring embarrassment to their king from this point forward."

As we walk back to the passageway and I calm down, I start to feel bad for the troll I had drug back to his King. Not bad enough to regret doing it but still felt bad knowing their punishments were usually cruel and very painful. At least I am confident knowing that this incident would spread quickly and we should have no further instances of this kind.

When we step through the passageway Penelope instantly wraps me in a hug. "Thank you. I have been telling them that it is not acceptable but until you were here, they wouldn't listen. I thought that since you needed some sleep and were going to get here late, it would actually help when you caught one of them doing something like that."

I felt something tap my leg. I look down and see the goblin that had been being pushed by the troll.

She is wringing her hands in a nervous gesture. "I am sorry you had to help me. I wanted to make sure you know I am thankful you helped though. I don't want to cause you any inconvenience with my troubles."

I smile. "It was no trouble. I don't think anyone should be treated like that and I intend to make sure that while you are in our realm, you are treated respectfully. That behavior was unacceptable and will not be tolerated here. It was no inconvenience to make sure you have an enjoyable trip here to our realm."

She grins proudly and walks to Rayne, with a new spring to her step, and is led to the portal she needs to get to her first destination.

When Rayne gets back, she looks at me with her arms crossed over her chest and a scowl on her face. "You so have to teach me how you did that rising in the air thing. That was so cool. I can't believe you kept that to yourself!"

I frown. "I didn't even know I was doing it. I was so mad that it just kinda happened. I must have been using the air to create some kind of stairs to rise up like that."

"So, how did the Troll King take you barging in pissed off and telling him off?"

I look over at Chase and he stares back expressionless. Apparently, I am on my own on this one. I huff out a breath. "He was pretty pissed off at his troll. Unfortunately, their punishments are cruel and painful, but I didn't have a choice. I had to make sure they knew that kind of thing was not allowed here whether I am here or not."

She laughs. "That one deserved it. That is not the first time we have had that kind of problem with him. He thought since you weren't here and didn't personally see him do it you wouldn't do anything about it. We tried telling him you didn't care if you had seen it and as soon as we told you about it you would have the same reaction. It just happened you saw it and the reaction was so much more satisfying than we ever could have imagined."

I roll my eyes. "You know it's usually not a good thing when someone is going to be punished in a cruel and painful way. I still don't regret taking him back there and telling off the King. It will keep the other trolls a more leery of crossing us. It might help to slow down what they are planning with the faeries. If we can keep them a little hesitant it will give us time to stop them."

"Speaking of the faeries, wait until you see their newest method of breaking through our defenses, you are going to have a fit."

I snap my head around with my face lips pursed in anger. "What are they up to now?"

"They have resorted to trying to seduce us. It's actually pretty funny. We have been playing along to pass the time. We let them think they might actually have a chance and that their flirting might be working and then they slowly figure out we are messing with them."

I'm not sure how to react to that. "I can see how that can be fun but are you making matters worse? We don't want to piss them off to the point where they are going to try and retaliate."

"They don't get offended. They take it as a challenge to see if they can actually get one of us to sincerely respond to them."

I look at Chase with a smirk. "In that case, it could be really fun. It would definitely give us some insight into what they are planning. If they keep stepping up their game trying to win one of us, then one of them is eventually going to say something that will help us figure out what they are up to. They won't be able to help but to brag and try to make it sound innocent. We already know they are up to something so when they say something like that thinking we don't have a clue about what's going on then they will actually be telling us more than they realize."

Landon smiles proudly at me. "Good job. You figured out what our plan was before we had to spell it out for you."

I stick my tongue out at him knowing he is teasing me.

CHAPTER 13

The next morning, we get everything set up and are ready when the passageways open. A really pretty faerie girl is the first one through. She spots Chase and sashays her way over to him.

I can't help but smile as I silently follow her. Chase is smiling at me behind her but she doesn't know I am there so she thinks he is smiling at her. She stops in front of him and looks up at him. "I haven't seen you before."

He smirks. "I have been with my wife on a little trip."

She makes a pouty face. "You are too young to be tied down to one girl. You should have all your options available to you. You would have so much more fun with a faerie girl than a witch."

Chase winks at me behind her and she gets bolder, thinking he was winking at her. She steps up close and starts to put her finger on his chest. The problem is she can't get to his chest. Her finger stops about an inch away from him and she can't get any closer.

He leans down and whispers, "Nobody besides my wife is allowed to touch me like that."

She spins on her heel and sees me standing there smiling at her. She looks back and forth between us. Then she smirks. "Alright, I can see you have already been informed about the challenge. One of us will get one of you it is just a matter of time."

I step to the side to let her pass. "It's always good to have dreams."

She sashays off and Chase grabs my hips and pulls me back up against him. A shiver runs down my spine as he whispers in my ear. "I miss our beach."

I smile at him over my shoulder and join the others.

The rest of the day goes smoothly. We don't have any more problems with the trolls or the faeries. It seems they are watching to see the dynamic while we are all together. They are used to Chase and I not being here and want to see how different things are now that we are back. It is starting to look like they aren't sure what to think about things running exactly the same.

While we are waiting for the next arrival, I voice my observations. "I think that in the other realms when the leader is away the other Guardians behave differently. It seems to confuse the trolls and faeries that things are run the same whether I am here or not. That makes me think to them it is just a job they have to do. With us it is something we care about and we are all so close that we don't have to have constant approval from anyone."

Landon agrees. "I was noticing that too. It was like they were trying to scope it out and couldn't figure out what had changed. They were desperately looking for something that could be considered a weakness. Now that they are starting to realize that we truly are a team they are not sure what to do."

Penelope sighs. "How horrible living like that must be. Not knowing who you can trust and knowing that any person you come into contact with will throw you under the bus if it will benefit them. I couldn't imagine a life where I always have to be looking over my shoulder to make sure no one is trying to shove a knife in my back."

Rayne smirks. "What they really don't understand is that is what will make the difference in the end. We may be more powerful than them but our bond and our trust in each other is what will make sure that we win. While they are looking for ways to sacrifice each other to gain the most, we will be here making sure that no harm comes to any of us. They will fight amongst themselves when the time comes and we will come together seamlessly."

Ethan pulls her over on his lap and gives her a sweet kiss. She flips us all off as we all say, "Aww."

I freeze as I feel something that I can't place. Chase instantly turns to me when he feels the shift in my emotions. He studies my face. "What is going on?"

I pry my eyes away from the spot in the trees and the look in my eyes has him by my side in seconds. I look back at the trees. I can feel something there. It is cold and feels like pure evil. I can't explain the feeling but it is even worse than when Dalton and Kynzie had been taken over by the darkness. This is something that has come from another realm and it is more evil than I have ever felt in one place.

I search the trees for anything that doesn't belong there. I can't see anything except for the trees and plants that have always been there. I can hear Chase trying to say something to me but it sounds like he is talking to me through a tunnel. I can hear his voice faintly but not what he is saying. I am so focused on trying to see what is there that nothing else matters at that moment.

I can feel the presence is amused with my focus. Then it is gone as fast as it came. I look at Chase and he catches me as my legs give out.

"Baby, talk to me. What happened?"

I shake my head to clear it from the fog that had taken over. "I'm not exactly sure what happened. I do know that something crossed over into our realm that does not belong here. It is clever and cunning and the most evil presence that I have ever felt."

They instantly whip their heads around to the spot where

I had been staring. "It's gone. It's fast. I didn't even feel it until it was already in the trees. I couldn't see anything only feel it. It was amused that I was focused so much on it that I couldn't hear what you were saying. At least that was what I think amused it until it was suddenly gone and my head was all foggy."

Chase furrows his brow. "What do you mean your head was all foggy?"

"I'm not sure how to explain it. Almost like waking up from a dream that seems so real and it takes you a minute to figure out where you are and that you were dreaming. When you're not able to think clearly and feel like you are in a fog."

The others looked at each other with worried looks. I don't blame them. I am just as worried as they are. "Do you think it was in my head?"

They exchange another look before Chase responds. "It sounds like it. The question is what was it looking for and what did it find funny?"

"No, the question is how is it going to use whatever it found and how do we stop it? We can't even see it I can sense it and know where it is but we can't risk firing anything at it in case it doesn't have a solid form. This is evil unlike anything this realm has ever dealt with. We need to figure out where it came from and what it is."

Just as I finish saying that I feel the presence of more witches. I look around worried about what is there and let out a sigh of relief when I see our parents standing there with worried expressions on their faces.

Dad looks at me on the ground with Chase and furrows his brow. "What happened? We felt something so strong come from here we know that you had to have combined your powers and draw from the Origin."

I am shaking my head before he is finished. "It wasn't us." I explain to them what happened. Their worried looks get more intense the further into the story I get.

Derek is wracking his brain trying to think of anything he has read in his studies that would give us any kind of clue as to what had just come through the portal. Finally, he looks up with a shocked look on his face.

I glance around at the others and see my anxious expression mirrored on all of their faces. When I turn back to Derek his shocked expression has turned to one of horror.

I instantly shoot up to my feet. "What is it? I can see that you know what happened."

He opens and closes his mouth with no sound for a couple of minutes before he is finally able to speak. "I had completely forgotten about it. I should have told you to lock that realm's passageway. All the other realms have that passageway to where it can be entered from their realm but none can enter from the other realm."

We stare at him confused waiting for him to elaborate. When he doesn't Chase nudges him. "You have to be more specific. We have no idea what you are talking about."

He takes a deep breath before beginning. "There is a realm called the shadows. That is where all the realms banish any of their dark souls and the pieces of darkness they remove from children. Darkness can seep into any realm. It will attach to anything that will sustain it. When it is removed from a soul, it is sent to the realm of the shadows. All the other realms have it set up to where they can send anyone or anything into the realm of shadows but nothing from the realm of shadows can enter their realm. I didn't even remember about that realm until just now."

He snaps his head over to me with a look of panic. "Annisa, right now you have to focus on the realm of shadows. You will be able to feel the cold and the evil coming from it. Then you have to close that passageway. Don't let anything else from there in our realm."

I instantly close my eyes and reach out to the passageways. I immediately feel what he was talking about. I also feel another presence making his way to our realm. I push that presence back to where it came from and firmly close that passageway. No other beings are going to be coming through there.

When I open my eyes, I nod so everyone knows I have closed the passageway. "I was able to push the being trying to come through back and close the passageway. There were so many of them waiting to come through. If we hadn't been here, our realm would have been overrun."

Chase looks at me. "No, if you hadn't been here. None of us had any clue that it was even here. You were the only one that could sense it."

My mom interrupts. "We could feel the power but not what was creating it. Like we said when we got here, we thought it was you guys trying to fight something."

I let out a frustrated breath. "I don't know if we will be strong enough to fight this one. Even with combining our power and drawing from the Origin, I don't know if it will be enough."

Their eyes snap to me shocked. "It was able to get inside my head and make me focus on nothing but it while it rummaged around looking for whatever it wanted and I didn't even know. It was cold, pure evil and very powerful."

Nobody knows what to say about that. My dad voices his suggestion. "Well, first we have to figure out how we are going to find it and then we will see if you have enough power on your own. If not, there is something we haven't told you that will make all the difference."

We stare at him surprised.

He sighs. "We were hoping to never have to tell you this because you didn't need it. Seeing as how you are our direct descendants, we are able to loan you our power in times of great need. If it comes down to you combining your power and drawing from the Origin and it is still not enough, we can channel our power through each of you to give you the added push that you need. It can only be used if the outcome of you losing will result in catastrophic consequences in this realm."

I sigh. "I think letting something that evil loose in this realm would qualify. I also know how to find it. You said you felt the power and assumed it was us. Now that you know its not us you can focus on that power and know where it is."

Dad smiles at me. "That is a good idea. I'm sorry but we can't let that thing run loose in this realm so we will stay here and guard the passageways and you will have to go after it now. We will create a portal to where it is. Remember you don't have to defeat it you just have to weaken it enough so Annisa can force it back to its own realm."

CHAPTER 14

They concentrate for so long that I am starting to think they can't find it. When they finally open their eyes, Mom raises her eyebrows. "Damn that thing is fast. We had to watch and get its pattern down so we could put you in front of where it's going. Be careful it feeds off the emotions of people so it will only get stronger the longer it is here. Now go before it gets past."

We run for the portal and emerge in the middle of a field. I have no idea where we are and no time to try and figure it out. I can feel the presence coming our way very fast. I point in the direction it is coming from. We combine our power, draw from the Origin, and create a wall.

I know the instant the presence hits the wall. I can feel it but what is really creepy is the power from the magick that has stopped it takes away its ability to blend into the background. It hits the wall and becomes a black spot on the wall. We take the wall and circle it around so it creates a bubble around the presence.

Then we hear the weirdest sound we have ever heard. It starts to laugh. As it laughs, my blood turns cold and I shiver. The others have a similar reaction.

From the tone of the voice I am able to determine the presence is male. He even has a creepy voice. "You think your puny little bubble can hold me? I am not one that can be banished so easily. I let you stop me so I could draw power from your magick."

As he is talking, he is getting bigger and our bubble is growing thinner. He is drawing the magick out of the bubble and taking it into himself. We immediately withdraw our magick to stop feeding him and making him stronger.

He laughs again. "You have no chance of defeating me. I will feed off of you and then nobody will be able to banish me. If I have your power, then I will be unstoppable.

I can feel him trying to draw our magick out. He keeps trying to pull harder and harder when it is not leaving us.

Rayne smirks. "Not as cocky now are you? You really think we are going to let you come to our realm, take our magick and then go terrorize innocent people?"

He doesn't say anything but his efforts double. It seems he is unable to draw our magick out of us but if we use it against him he is able to absorb it. I am desperately trying to figure out how we will be able to weaken him to get him back in his realm without using our magick against him.

Then a thought hits me. I open up the connection to talk to the others hoping he won't be able to get in our heads and overhear us. *"Make sure you create a wall around your mind so he can't get in."*

They confirmed they have already done that. *"Good, now keep him distracted. I am going to open the portal to the shadow realm but I am going to do it in a way that creates a vacuum. If our parents put their power into it, then it should be a strong enough vacuum to suck him back through. As long as we are not using our magick against him directly he can't absorb it but I want to get the vacuum created before he realizes what we are doing and takes off. If he keeps traveling as fast as he was there will be no way to get him to stop long enough to create the vacuum."*

Rayne starts to laugh. "You think we would give up our power to you? Don't you know it's rude to come to another realm and take anything you want without being invited or offered anything?"

He is getting frustrated with not being able to draw our power out. He keeps inching closer hoping if he gets close enough it will work. He is so focused on drawing out our power and Rayne taunting him that he never even realizes I am opening a passageway right behind him.

When he feels the air around him start to get pulled back into the vacuum I have created, he laughs again. "You really think you can just suck me back into that realm? I am stronger and faster than you."

Just as he is about to take off at his super fast speed the vacuum gets significantly stronger. He is being pulled and is not able to pull himself out of it. "No, this can't happen. I am stronger than you."

I laugh. "Apparently not or you wouldn't be going back to where you came from. Just to be clear no one from your realm is welcome here and this passageway will be closed so no others can escape."

He is sucked back through the passageway and I close it firmly. We then step back through the portal to where our parents are waiting for us.

I sit down exhausted. "Thank you for your help. I think it was your help that prevented him from being able to draw our power out of us and to create a strong enough vacuum to suck him back to his own realm."

Mom leans down and gives me a hug. "That was a really good idea. I am so proud of all of you. You figured it out very quickly that he was able to absorb the magick you used against him and didn't give him any more power. Honestly, I was at a loss on how to defeat him without using magick against him. That was very smart to use the vacuum."

"Thanks mom. Do you guys mind staying for a little bit while we recoup a little?"

"Sure honey, you kids all sit and rest for a little bit. We will stay and help out for a couple of hours."

We sit down in the chairs we have set up, relax, and try to

get some of our energy back. We have just settled in when a faerie comes through the passageway. He looks over at us with a smirk.

"Oh, did the all-powerful Annisa forget about the passageway to the shadow realm? I thought you had everything under control and wouldn't tolerate beings from other realms behaving in a way you didn't approve of."

I lift my head and look him in the eyes. "I do and I won't tolerate bad behavior in this realm. That's why the shadow that found its way here has been sent back to the shadow realm and the passageway closed."

His jaw drops. "You banished the most powerful shadow spirit within an hour of it coming to your realm? That's impossible. Nobody could banish him that quickly. You would have had to gather so many more to have the power needed to banish him."

I smile sweetly at him. "I guess you are going to have to try to find something else to distract me so you can try to do whatever it is you are up to. I know what you are doing and it won't work. I didn't have to gather anyone. We are powerful enough to face anything you throw at us all while still keeping an eye on you and what you are up to. Now I think your trip to our realm has been cut short, and it's time for you to head home."

He looks at me with disbelief. He then looks around at the others to see if I am bluffing. When he sees the bored expressions on their faces, he knows I am telling him the truth. He spins on his heel and disappears through the passageway back to the faerie realm.

Dad starts to laugh. "Sweetheart, you really shouldn't taunt them like that. They are still adjusting and trying to figure out what they can get away with and what they can't."

I grin mischievously. "I know, dad, but I want to make sure they know they can't get away with anything. If they know they have to follow our rules then it will make it harder for them to do whatever they are trying to do. We all know they are here to recruit and gather an army. It's our job to prevent that and protect all the realms from them. What good is having all this power if we don't use it to help others?"

He smiles at me proudly. "I understand what you are saying but what you aren't taking into consideration is that you are showing them your strength up front. They will know exactly what they are up against and you will have nothing left to throw a curve ball with."

I think about that for a moment. "That is partially true. Once they figure out I used a vacuum to banish the shadow instead of magick, they will think we didn't have enough magick to do it. It won't occur to them we figured out he could absorb magick used against him. They assume we are still learning and we don't know much about the other realms. That's why he told the shadow realm they could slip in. He didn't expect the shadow to want us as a trophy. He figured the shadow would evade us and not come near us and when it did it would drain our power. They will think we got lucky because the shadow got cocky."

"Ok, good point. I still want you to be careful. The more you show them up the more determined they are going to be to prove they are better. If it is a constant battle of the wills nobody wins. Sometimes you have to sit back and observe. You will be amazed at what you can learn by watching people. You will eventually start to be able to predict their moves and figure out their process of thinking and how they come to the conclusions that they do. Once you have that information it becomes natural for you to counter the moves that come natural to them."

"Ok, but we can't follow them around and watch them. We have to be here and monitor and protect."

He crosses his arms over his chest. "I never said follow them around. Observe them when they are here interacting with you. Everybody changes their behavior based on who they are around. What you need to observe is how they behave when they are interacting with you. Instead of teasing the faeries with false hope of what they see is a challenge, watch how they interact with each of you. You will start to see a pattern. Are they doing this to distract you? Are they drawing all of your attention to the one they are attempting to seduce so they can sneak undocumented faeries into this realm that are able to explore with nobody knowing they are here? There has to be a reason behind this challenge."

I perk up at the last part. "I never even thought about the fact that they could try to sneak other faeries through the passageway. We wouldn't notice because so many are coming and going that I wouldn't feel someone coming through that was not scheduled to. We will all position ourselves tomorrow so we have a view of the passageway and still pretend to be watching the faerie try their luck. If we are not directly watching the passageway, they will probably still sneak in. Penelope, you are the one that can blend in the best and you are silent walking through these woods. If one sneaks through follow them and don't let them see you."

Landon starts to say something but I don't give him the chance. "Landon, she will not approach them or talk to them. They won't know she is there. She is going to follow them and see where they are going and what they are doing. If she gets in trouble, all she has to do is open the connection and we can be at her side in an instant."

He nods his head but didn't look happy at all about it as he furrows his brow and his jaw clenches. Chase doesn't appear pleased either as his back goes rigid. I roll my eyes at their show of protection. "Look guys, we have power of our own and we don't always need you looking over our shoulders trying to protect us. We know you want to protect us but sometimes you have to let us do our thing. You know Penelope is the best one for this so you will have to deal with it and get over it."

CHAPTER 15

The next day I am determined to figure out what the faeries are up to. When we get to the clearing, we rearrange the chairs so no matter whom the faeries approach the rest of the group will be able to keep an eye on the portal with their peripheral vision. All I can do is hope they don't go after Penelope. We need her to be free to follow the faeries sneaking in.

When the passageway opens, a good-looking faerie comes through from his realm. He looks around and when he sees me he gives me a cocky smirk. He approaches me with what could only be called a strut. You can tell he is used to getting any woman he wants. He is used to the faerie women falling all over themselves for the chance to be with him. I smile thinking how much fun it will be shooting him down.

When he gets to me I realize I will not be able to watch the passageway without him seeing what I am doing. I have to trust the others to keep an eye on it while I keep the cocky faerie distracted.

His cocky smirk stays in place as he stops right in front of me. "Now that you see what the faerie realm has to offer you are probably regretting tying yourself to that witch. I can help you out with that little problem."

I raise my eyebrows. "Really and how do you propose to do that?"

"One night with me and you will forget all about any other man. You will be ready to end your marriage and follow me back to the faerie realm."

I laugh. "Why, would I want to leave the man I love and that loves me for someone that will ditch me for the next opportunity to get someone else in bed?"

He cocks his eyebrows. "If I had a real woman like you, I wouldn't need to look for pleasures from others. It's not my fault they have all been lacking while I was waiting for you to come into my life."

I can't help it I burst out in a full belly laugh. "Wow, you really are quite cocky. Sorry, but I have absolutely no interest in you at all."

He furrows his brow. "That's not possible. All women would give up their most prized possession for the chance to be with me."

I roll my eyes. "Just because you parade yourself in front of the lonely and desperate women instead of the ones that are looking for something meaningful does not mean you are irresistible to all women. In fact, you are repulsive to most."

He glares at me and stalks off into the trees. Rayne is laughing as she leads him to the portal that will take him to his first destination.

I glance around at the others and find that Penelope is gone and Landon is scowling. I sigh as I realize we had been right, and they have been distracting us so they could sneak faeries in without us knowing.

I look over at Chase. "I wonder how many they have got through without us knowing. We could face quite a few undocumented faeries here."

"It looks like they are being cautious about it. Only one came through. Nobody else even stuck their head through to see if they could make it. I think they are just bringing one every once in a while. I don't think it is every time or we would have figured it out by now."

Suddenly Penelope opens the connection and Landon takes off in the direction she had gone. He stops when he hears what she wants to let us know.

"They are so cocky that they never even checked to see if anyone was following them. I have been able to stay close enough to hear them but they haven't noticed me or even looked around. It's almost like they think once they get out of the clearing they are home free."

Landon visibly relaxes at hearing she has not been discovered and it is not likely she will be.

She continues. *"It looks like they are all meeting at a cabin in the mountains somewhere. It is really remote and not much around it. There is a small town not far from here. When they take the portal out of the clearing there is another one set up right next to it, they can take to the cabin. I'm not sure how they created the portal. All I can figure is that one of them knows how to do it and didn't let us know about it."*

I am seething. "I don't think they would have wanted us to know about that. Since there is nothing in the contract about them not creating their own portals, we can't do anything about that. However, we can do something about them bringing in faeries without our knowledge or approval."

"Hold on, I think we need to keep an eye on them. If we don't let them know that we have figured this out we will be able to figure out what they are doing if we are able to watch them without them knowing about it. I can hear them in the cabin. They are planning a trip soon. They are only waiting for one more to get here then they are going to meet up with someone they know is here and has been waiting a long time for the passageways to be opened."

"How could the faerie that was brought through possibly know the passageways would be opened in his lifetime? For that matter, how did he know they would ever be opened? When the Origin brought them over it didn't give them a detailed report on what was going to happen."

"It seems like the faeries figured out the Origin always pulled people for the same general spot and they placed faeries there they wanted on this side so when the passageways eventually opened they would have faeries they knew would cooperate in their cause here. They are all trying to figure out how many children the one they are visiting first had managed *to father. It sounds like their intention was to send these faeries here with the sole purpose of creating hybrids. We really need to figure out why the hybrids are so important."*

"Ok, give me a mental picture of where you are and I will create a portal back here. I think we have gotten what we can for now. We will have to wait for the next one to come through and follow them from there."

She steps through the portal and smiles proudly at Landon. "See, no problem. I knew I could do it without being seen. I didn't even need to use the air trick to create a diversion if they started to suspect someone was there."

I look at her with a confused expression. "What air trick?"

"Landon and I discussed last night different ways I could distract the faeries if they thought they were being followed. We came up with the idea that if they started to look in my direction that I could use the air to rustle some leaves or cause something to fall so they would investigate in that direction instead."

I grin. "That is a great idea. Keep that in mind when you follow the next one tomorrow."

Landon scowls but doesn't say anything. He knows he is going to be outvoted and Penelope will go no matter what he says about it. He doesn't like it but he also doesn't have a logical argument against it.

Chase gives him a sympathetic look. "She will be fine. She is smart and quick. Even if she is spotted, she will be able to get away before they can get to her. She knows to give Annisa a mental picture and Annisa will immediately create a portal and ask questions later."

Landon nods. Chase's words don't comfort him but he is a little more confident in Penelope's ability to get away because of them. He is still going to worry but at least it won't eat away at him.

The rest of the day passes pretty quietly. The trolls are overly polite trying to make sure they don't give me any reason to report them to their King. I can only imagine the punishment the overly confident troll had to face when I turned him in and from the reaction of the other trolls it seems I really don't want to know the details. I shudder at the possibilities.

I come to really enjoy when the elves and goblins come through. They are always nice and ask questions that will help them get the most out of their visit. They seem to really treasure the opportunity to come here and learn about our realm. Of course, every goblin that comes through is so grateful for us getting rid of the stench in their realm that they would have done anything we asked of them.

The last traveler of the day is a little goblin woman. She looks up at us with pure awe on her face. "You are the ones that helped us. I can't believe you greet the travelers yourselves. I am so honored to meet you."

I chuckle. "We are just normal witches. There is no reason for us to have someone else out here to greet our travelers. We quite enjoy meeting all of you."

"But you are so powerful that you could do what nobody else has ever done. You must have more important tasks you could do rather than greeting lowly beings such as me."

I hate the way the other realms have made the goblins feel like they aren't worth anything. "We are no better than you. We simply have different gifts is all. I'm sure there are things you can do that we would not be able to. We don't believe there is anyone who is not worth our time."

"I thank you for your kind words. Can I ask a question of you?"

"Of course, ask anything you want."

"My brother is one that was brought here before the passageways were opened. I would like to find him. Do you know where I might begin looking?"

"I'm sorry. I wish I could help you. Unfortunately, we don't know where any of the beings are that were brought over before the passageways opened or why they were brought over or where they came through. All I can suggest is to look in places that you feel he would want to stay in and would be comfortable in."

She smiles at me. "That was my intention. I have scheduled my tour with that thought in mind. I am hoping to get lucky and find him while traveling. We were quite close before he was taken so I am hoping that will help me to be able to feel if he is near."

I smile at her. "I wish you luck and hope when we see you next on your way home you will have found your brother."

She waves and follows Ethan to her portal. After she has gone through I wonder aloud, "I never even thought about the family members who might be missing the ones that were brought over. It must be hard to have one of your family members simply vanish one day. I always thought about how hard it must have been for the beings when they were brought here with no knowledge of this realm or how to blend in but it never occurred to me they would be missed at home."

Penelope is looking at the spot where the little goblin woman had disappeared. "I hope she finds her brother. It must have been so hard to be separated from him and not be able to even talk to him."

CHAPTER 16

Apparently, the faeries have taken to trying for Rayne the most. She has become the biggest challenge with her attitude. While she is playing along with the faerie that has approached her today I watch as a faerie sneaks her head through the portal to make sure it is clear for her to come through. When she sees us all looking at Rayne, she slips through and takes off into the trees with Penelope close behind her.

It is only a couple of minutes after the faerie has snuck through that the one talking to Rayne lets himself be led to the portal he is scheduled to go through. We continue to monitor the comings and goings while Penelope spies on the faeries and tries to figure out where they are going. She gives periodic updates as she follows them.

Landon is handling her being gone and following them better than I expected. I think her updates are more for his peace of mind more than anything else. Just when he would start to get anxious because we hadn't heard from her in a while she would send an update. I think she is monitoring his emotions and using them as a guide as to when she needed to send an update.

The longer it goes and the more they travel the more confused I get. I can't figure out why they are going from portal to portal and not staying in one place for very long. Either they don't know where the faeries are that they are looking for or they are trying to make sure nobody is following them. I am starting to wonder if they know Penelope is there.

All of a sudden Penelope sends me picture of where she is and I create a portal. She comes through with a shocked look on her face. Landon is instantly by her side checking and making sure she is not hurt in any way. She is looking at me with wide eyes and patiently waiting for him to be done so she can tell us what she had seen.

Finally, Landon determines she is fine and stops fussing over her. She rolls her eyes at him. "I told you they would never know I was there. They were trying to make sure nobody knew where they were going and that is why they used so many portals. Apparently, there are faeries that can track someone through the portals. They were creating a web and even backtracking a few times to make it to difficult for them to be tracked. They were not as quick as they thought they were and I was able to slip through each portal before they closed them. They never had any idea I was there."

I furrow my brow. "Then why did you send that image like with urgency to get you back. I thought you had been discovered."

"I almost wish I had been discovered rather than found what they were doing. They are making it to where they can't be tracked because they don't want anyone to find the village they were going to. I have a clear image of what it looks like so we can get there any time we need to but I don't know where it is. We will have to get there by portal."

"Ok, that's not a problem but what is so important about this village?"

"All the faeries and trolls that have been brought over are there. They have taken wives and sometimes kidnapped women and made them slaves. They have created an army of hybrids. What's even worse is that they have raised them to believe that the humans are beneath them. They have shown them how weak they think the humans are which is proven by the ones that have been held captive all this time. They have been training them since birth to be an army for them."

As she talks my stomach starts to knot up. By the time she is done I have a huge knot of anxiety sitting in my gut. This is not what I was expecting. I am suddenly glad to have the assistance that was offered to us by the magickal creatures.

I am frantically trying to figure out what to do. "Well it is only the faeries and the trolls so we still have hope of help from the elves and goblins. Also, there have to be some of the hybrids that are not happy with one of their parents being treated like that. They might go through the motions of what they are being taught and waiting for an opportunity to free their other parent. We might still get some help from some of them."

Penelope has been nodding while I speak. "I stayed on the outskirts of the village for a couple of hours trying to get a feel for the hybrids. They are very powerful. It seems the human blood enhances the magick of the faeries and trolls. Once that information gets back to the Faerie King we are going to have a real problem on our hands. The children all go along with what they are being taught but they all look like robots. Their hearts are not in it. There are a few that are excited about it but the majority seem to do the least of what is expected of them. I get the feeling they are punished if they don't behave in the manner they are taught."

"That could work in our favor. We have to find a way to keep that information from the Faerie King. I just don't know how. There really doesn't seem to be a way to keep it from him unless when the hybrids are faced with him they refuse to show their true power. I don't see that happening if they are programmed to behave in a certain manner. I also know the faeries that are here will tell the King about the hybrids. We may be able to keep the hybrids here but we have no control over keeping the faeries here. The only factor in our behavior is that we have no documentation of them coming through the portal so we will be able to delay their return because of that. But we still have the problem of the ones that are documented going back and letting the King know what is going on."

Landon interrupts. "We need to find the goblins and elves that were brought over and see what the situation is with them. We need to know what all we are dealing with."

Penelope smiles. "I heard one faery say they had their own village not far from there. Apparently, they banded together for support and to not feel so alone in this realm. The faeries and trolls laughed at the other beings coming together simply for friendship and not a bigger goal. They believe the other beings to be weak because they are not manipulating the powerful hybrids for their own gain. They think because they treat their human mates with respect and create families that they are wasting any potential the hybrids might have."

"That means they will underestimate the power of those hybrids. The good part of this whole thing is that someone fighting to protect those they love will fight so much harder than one that is being forced to do as ordered. They will have more heart and a very strong motivator to keep them going."

I scowl. "I don't think it is ever a good thing to ask a child to fight against their parents no matter how badly they were treated. I agree the ones that were shown love will fight with all they have while the others will fight for a cause but I don't think that it is fair to make a child choose between its parents. We will essentially say to the hybrids of the faeries and trolls that they have to choose to either fight for their magickal parent that has mistreated their human parent or to fight for the human parent who has been mistreated."

Rayne rolls her eyes. "No, we will tell them they have to choose if they want to fight for what they want or what they are told to fight for. It will come down to what each of the hybrids wants on which side they will fight on. If they truly believe the faeries and trolls are wrong, then they will fight against that and if they have bought into the notion that they have been taught then they will fight on that side. It will be a personal decision for each hybrid. You also have to take into consideration that some of the hybrids of the elves and goblins will fight with the faeries and trolls. They might feel like they are better than the humans and fall in with that side even though it was not drilled into them since birth."

I nod my head. "You're right. There will be some from each village on each side. We can only hope that when they are faced with someone they have always considered a friend, it will cause them to pause and think about what they are doing. That might be all it takes for some of them to switch to our side."

"Always the optimist, you haven't taken into consideration that it could be all it takes for them to go to the other side."

I sigh. "I considered it I didn't think that it needed to be said. We really need to get a better feel for the other village. Penelope and Landon, can you go and scope it out? I will create a portal back to where you were and you can make your way to the other village from there."

Penelope and Landon both nod and step through the portal I created.

I sit down and try to figure out what our next move should be. I know I can't let the hybrids go to the faerie and troll realms but I have no idea how to prevent it.

As I chew on my bottom lip while trying to figure it all out Chase comes up behind me and starts to rub my shoulders. "Baby, you don't have to figure it all out right away by yourself. We will figure out what to do after we have more information. Once Penelope and Landon get back, we will sit down and talk about it all. There is a solution—we just have to figure out what it is. They will not show up today and demand to take the hybrids to their realms so we have some time."

"I am just afraid they are going to try and sneak the

hybrids by us using the same system they used to get the faeries here. If they think they could get by unnoticed to get here, then they will think they can get back that way too. We will have to stop them before they make it to the passageway and have a reason to delay them from leaving."

"Since we already know to watch the passageway and that their distraction doesn't work anymore we will be able to catch any of them trying to sneak through to take the hybrids to their realm. There are many ways we can delay their departure. Only the ones that have been documented as coming through would be able to go back without a problem. As for them taking a hybrid with them, well we have our system set up to prevent them from taking anyone that doesn't want to go. That system takes a while to complete. We did that on purpose to make sure the person going has time to think about what they are doing so they don't regret the decision to go."

I sigh. "I know but if they are being forced to do this, then they will complete the process so they won't get punished. I know the system should work in theory but for the ones that truly believe in their cause and want to go and fight for the Faerie King will be able to get through."

"Yes, but wouldn't you rather they were over in the faerie realm instead of here where they could harm innocent people? Over there they will no longer be the star student they will be the hybrid. I think it will not be as easy a transition as they think. The hybrids are going to go over there with the attitude that they are better than everyone else and that will be a huge problem for the arrogant faeries and trolls that are full blooded. They will feel they are better than the hybrids and will not accept them so readily like it is believed."

I think about that. "I think you're right. I got the distinct impression from the Faerie King he thought any being not full blooded is not the same and is simply a tool to be used. I don't think the hybrids will take it very well when they are treated the way they have always treated humans. I almost

wish I could be there to see what happens."
He laughs. "Me too."

CHAPTER 17

The elves and goblins are a little more observant of their surroundings. Landon and Penelope are discovered outside of the village. The good thing is they are welcomed into the village and are able to obtain a lot of useful information. They end up staying at the village overnight.

The next morning, I create a portal for them to return to the clearing. They are smiling and in a great mood.

Penelope can't contain her excitement. "I can't believe how great they are. Oh, and the goblin that was looking for her brother found him. They were so excited to be reunited and she was having a blast playing with her niece and nephew. It is the exact opposite of the other village. They are a community that all helps each other and the humans are treated like everyone else. There are a couple of goblins and elves that are raising the children on their own because the people they were with couldn't handle all the magick and weren't happy in the village. They could leave and sometimes even visit with their children. They would not allow any of the humans to take the hybrids out into the mortal world though. They wanted to make sure the kids were safe and were afraid if they were to be integrated with the mortal realm then they would accidentally do something that would expose them. They are all about protecting the children and not training them for any specific task. They all know their history from both realms. It is a true blend of this realm and theirs."

I can't help but smile. It is exactly the situation we were hoping for when all of this started with one exception. I was hoping the children would be able to live in either realm without restriction. I don't like that they are so isolated and not taught how to blend in to society here in this realm. That is something we are going to have to work on after this is all taken care of.

Landon loves Penelope's excitement and lets her tell us all about their experience in the village. When she is done, we are all pretty certain the hybrids in this village are just as powerful as the ones in the other village.

I sigh. "I know most of them will probably side with us but since they have been so isolated from anyone else in this realm some of them will have resentment for that. They will feel like they are being deemed not worthy of this realm. They won't see it was done to protect them, they will see it as them not being good enough."

Some of Penelope's excitement fades. I hate I have caused that, but I want to make sure she has a realistic view of the situation. She furrows her brow. "I never thought about it like that. I can see what you are saying. I was writing up the attitude that some of them had as them being teenagers. It never occurred to me it could be so much more. Either way though, I think we can count on the support of most of them, even if some of them choose the other side. I also think if they go to the faerie and troll realms to join their cause they won't stay for long. If the faeries and trolls won't accept the hybrids of their own kind as being equals then the hybrids of elves and goblins are going to be at the bottom of the barrel for them. They are not used to the military style training lifestyle like the faeries and trolls are and they won't do well in that situation when they get there."

"That could cause a big problem because I don't see the faeries and trolls letting them leave if they don't like it there. We might have to do a rescue mission at some point to free the ones that changed their minds after they got there. It will give them a good motivator of wanting revenge but it can also cause them to be careless. That is a situation we will have to figure out as we go. It will be difficult but they have to make the choice for themselves. I refuse to keep any of them from joining whichever side they feel they need to be on."

Rayne rolls her eyes. "If they chose the other side then why are we going to rescue them? They are the ones that are deciding to work with the ones trying to take over realms they have no business taking over and we are going to rescue them when they don't get treated the way they wanted to. I say we let them sit there until the whole thing is over and then go for them."

I sigh. "We gave you another chance after you had chosen to fight for the wrong side. I think you need to have a little compassion and realize some people don't realize what they are getting themselves into and are fascinated with an idea until it comes time to execute that idea."

She nods her head, frowning, knowing I am right and not having an argument to refute what I had said.

Before we can say anything else, a faerie comes through the portal to go back to their realm. His trip has come to an end, and he is ready to go back to his own realm. The problem is he has a girl with him. It appears he is trying to pass her off as a human that wants to go live with him in the faerie realm. I can sense I am in the presence of a hybrid.

It is the first time I have come into contact with one. The feeling of them is unique. I can feel the powerful magick that she possesses but I can also feel the connection to the mortal realm. She gives no outward sign she is not who the faerie says she is except for the look of panic in her eyes. She definitely does not want to accompany him to the faerie realm. I am instantly very glad we have come up with our system to delay him from taking her.

I look at him. "We have a few procedures that must be completed before you will be allowed to take her to the faerie realm with you." While I am talking to him and watching the girl Chase has been watching the passageway.

Chase is suddenly gone from my side and has grabbed a hold of another faerie that is carrying an unconscious girl toward the passageway. Rayne and Penelope instantly step up to keep the faerie I was talking to from going anywhere as Ethan and Landon helped Chase bring the unconscious girl and the other faerie over.

I look at the faerie that was trying to sneak into the faerie realm and recognized him as one that had snuck in here. "It was very kind of you to lead us to the village where the hybrids are being kept but I can't allow you to take an unconscious girl to another realm without her saying she is in favor of going there."

I turn back to the faerie trying to distract me. "I also can't allow you to take this hybrid with you until I know for sure she is going willingly and not because she has been ordered to."

Rayne smirks. "Oh, will you look at that we are not as stupid as you thought we were? It must really suck to be played and beaten at your own game."

I roll my eyes at her. "We will not allow you to take the hybrids to your realm against their will."

The one I had been talking to stared at me defiantly. "You have no right to stop us from taking them. They belong in the faerie realm. They have faerie blood and need to be with their own kind. You have no claim on them."

I laugh. "I have more claim on them than you do. While they have faerie blood, they also have human blood. They were also raised in the human realm. That means they are of this realm and not yours. This is their home. If you were so adamant about taking them to your realm where you claim they belong then why did your King not put that in the contract? He never mentioned bringing the faerie hybrids to the faerie realm. If that was what he felt was right then he should have put it on the table during negotiations."

The girl glares at the man holding her by the arm. "You told us the Faerie King had fought for our right to live in your realm where we belong and he was denied and not given that option and that is why we had to sneak in."

The faerie looks around looking for any way out of his current situation. He is not smart enough to figure out that holding onto a teenage girl that is pissed and also has magick is not the best plan.

I can't stop the laugh that erupts from my chest when he goes flying through the forest and hits a tree. She crosses her arms over her chest and glares at him. The look of panic has disappeared from her eyes and now she has a stubborn look of defiance on her face.

She walks to where Chase has laid the unconscious girl on the ground. She puts her hand on the girl's forehead and closes her eyes. When she stands up the other girl wakes up and searches the area around her in confusion.

The one that had thrown the faerie against the tree looks at me with that same defiant look. "I want to go home and get my mother. I will take care of her somewhere else. We have been forced to train and my mother has been treated worse than a dog. She was expected to birth as many children as her body could handle and then discarded to care for the infants and toddlers until they could begin their training. I refuse to leave her and my brothers and sisters there with those crazy faeries."

I smile. "We will take care of it. I promise we will not leave them there to be treated like that."

I look around at the others and see they are uncomfortable with my statement. They don't think raiding the village right now is the best option.

I sigh. "I'm sorry guys but I can't leave them there. They need our help."

Ethan takes a deep breath. "I understand that but we are not prepared for this."

I smile as I open portals to the dwarves and the gnomes.

As the two creatures start to flood into the forest ready for battle, the others watch in shock. Chase shakes his head at my dramatics.

When they are all there, I close the portals and explain the situation to them. They listen intently and are ready to go as soon as I am done.

Drevin steps forward. "We will round up the faeries and trolls and bring them all back here bound to be dealt with. The hybrids and the humans can have the village to run as they see fit."

I smile to indicate my approval of the plan. I look over at the girl and see she is too distracted by the dwarves to really focus on anything that is going on. I laugh as I lead the girls to the portal that will lead us to the village.

I open the portal a little bit away from the village so we can get through and surround the village to hopefully prevent any of the faeries and trolls from escaping. As we are preparing I am surprised to find hybrids and goblins and elves from the other village.

I am met with smiling faces. One of the elves explains, "We could sense that something was happening here. As soon as all this magick was unleashed in this area we came to help."

I furrow my brow. "If you felt us arrive that means the faeries and trolls did too. We won't be able to surround them and surprise them. Some of them will get away."

She shakes her head. "Us elves are more in tune with the earth. We felt you because the land alerted us. They are too arrogant to listen to the land. They will have no idea you are here. They don't even keep watch on the perimeter of their village trusting that nobody would be foolish enough to mess with them."

I smile. "I guess they don't know what foolish is yet."

CHAPTER 18

We silently surround the village. It looks like the faeries and trolls are celebrating their beginning to return to their realms. They don't know they have been stopped before they have made their way through. I am amazed at the level of their arrogance in thinking nothing could have gone wrong.

We converge on the village at the same time. There is no break in our circle for anyone to slip through. The hybrids run to their mortal parents to try and protect them. They have been told since birth that if they were ever discovered that the other races would come in and kill everyone.

It doesn't take them long to realize we are avoiding the hybrids and the mortals and only focusing on the faeries and trolls. The hybrids are no longer holding defensive positions but are only watching to make sure they are out of the way and their mortal parents are not in the line of fire.

The faeries and trolls fight hard but they are no match for the forces we brought against them. It doesn't take long before all of them are bound and placed in an area to wait for us to decide what to do next.

I watch men and women walk past their children to spit in the faces of the faeries and trolls that had held them captive and forced them to live in these conditions.

I sigh when I see a small group of mortals and hybrids trying to sneak around the group so they could release their family member. I knew there were some that would not like what had happened. They are bound and placed along with the faeries and trolls they had been trying to release.

I look over at the group that is glaring at the bound captives. I'm not sure how to proceed from this point. One man in the group steps forward.

"We thank you for your assistance. Their magick is strong and they are masters at manipulating the mind and body to get what they want. You will want to be careful in how you interact with them."

I smile. "We are aware of their abilities. We will be taking them and sending them back to their realms to face their rulers and will be banned from ever entering this realm again. Is there any of you that wish to say a goodbye to any of them before they are gone and you will never see them again?"

They all glare at the ones that are bound and nobody makes a move to indicate they want a last goodbye. I am saddened by the idea that these children feel nothing for the parents that are being banished from this realm. None of them even want to say goodbye.

I look at the man that would most likely become the new leader in this village. "Is there anything you need from us? We are willing to help you in any way we can."

He studies me as if to determine how serious I am. "We would like to take our children and return to our world. We would appreciate it if you would not try and stop us from integrating back into the society of this realm."

I smile as the goblins and elves from the other village gasp. "I would like nothing more than for you to integrate back into the world. I don't believe keeping the hybrids isolated here is the best option. I leave it up to each of you whether you want to expose them to the rest of this realm or if you would rather stay here in this village. I will give you the same options as I am now offering to the goblins and elves.

Stay in your village or rejoin society whichever option you feel is best for your family. We will not interfere with that decision. I must stress how important it is for you to teach your children how to conceal their power and to mix into the society of this realm undetected. The world will not be kind to them if they expose who and what they are."

He looks over his shoulder before he responds. "I believe we will take a little time here in the village to teach them what they need to know to survive in the society and then we will go. I believe there may be some that will prefer to stay here but the majority will be leaving soon."

I nod to indicate I approve of his decision. The goblins and elves are watching them with interest. I laugh. "Please go and talk to them. You can all work together to decide what it is you want to do. You may want to combine your villages for those that wish to stay here and you may all decide to reemerge in society together so you all have a support group. Whatever decision you make is up to you. You have nothing to fear from us or the faerie or troll realms. I must warn the ones that want to stay here. The faeries and trolls do know how to find you. If you were to move on from here, it would be more difficult for them to locate you."

He looks around at the others again and it looks like they had not thought about the fact that other faeries and trolls could come here and try to take over. I figure if they decide they didn't want to integrate back into society then they could make another village in another location. That way it would be harder for them to be located.

I then turn and look at the faeries and trolls we had bound sitting on the ground. I am trying to figure out how we are supposed to get them all back to the clearing so we can send them back to where they came from.

Before I can voice my question the dwarves and elves start getting the faeries and trolls to their feet. Their legs are unbound so they can walk and they are guided through the portal I created back to the clearing.

Before I step through the portal, I give one last look at

the ones that are staying behind. It looks like they are attempting to make an uneasy peace. The mortals are untrusting of the goblins and elves. They are trying to show the mortals they have no intention of trying to take over their village and force them to do anything. I hope they will be able to work it out but there is nothing more for me to do here.

I step through the portal and am met with the angry glare of the faeries and trolls that are still bound. It looks like a couple of them have tried to run because they are dirty from being tackled to the ground and now their legs are bound from the hips to the ankles. It is a little excessive but I don't say anything about it.

I walk to each one and draw an 'x' on their foreheads. It doesn't leave a mark but they can feel the magick that is being placed on them as I finish each one. When I am done, I stand before the group.

"What I have done is place a powerful spell on you. If any of you try and enter our realm through any passageway at all you will be in excruciating pain until you leave and enter back into your home realm. If you leave and go to the realm of another being, you will continue to be in pain until you are back in your realm. I will leave it up to the other realms to decide if you will be allowed in their realm or not but if you try to get there by going through this one it will not work. It also will not work for you to go to another realm and try to enter this realm from there. The spell has been placed on each of you so no matter where you are coming from you will not be able to enter this realm. None of you are welcome here anymore and you will not be permitted back."

They look at me with mixed expressions. They have never heard of this and weren't sure if I am bluffing or not. They will find out soon enough when they try to sneak back in that I am most definitely not bluffing. When they cross over into this realm, they will feel like something is destroying them from the inside out. The excruciating pain will continue until they return to their home realm.

I nod my head and the dwarves toss the bound faeries

and trolls through the passageways back into their own realms. We do not unbind them before they are returned and we give no warning to the other realms that some of their people will be tossed through.

When they are done, I turn to the dwarves and gnomes. "I thank you for your assistance. I really appreciate that you came when we needed the help. Is there anything we can do to repay you?"

They both shake their heads and tell me they will come anytime we need them. I thank them again and create portals so they can return home.

As soon as they were gone I sigh. I can feel the Faerie King and his anger. He is about to step through the passageway and tell me exactly what he thinks of the treatment of his faeries.

Thankfully, our parents have been monitoring the situation and they appear seconds before the Faerie King steps through the passageway.

He glares at us all. "What is the meaning of tossing bound faeries through the passageway with no way to break their fall? They could have been seriously hurt due to your actions. I demand an explanation for this absurd behavior."

My dad steps forward, and he is just as angry as the Faerie King. "Your faeries have been holding mortals hostage and forcing them to bear children and to mate with them without the consent of the mortal. They have treated our mortals and the resulting children as slaves and training them for a war where they indicated the faerie and troll realms would take over and rule all realms. That behavior is in direct violation with the contract that you signed with us. I demand to know why I should not close the faerie realm passageway to this realm immediately and not allow any faeries access to this realm ever again."

The Faerie King sputters for a moment while he tries to find a way to respond that will not result with his entire race being banned from this realm. It looks like it takes a great deal of effort for him to say his next words.

"I didn't realize that was what was happening. I most certainly support your banishment of the faeries that were involved in this plot. I assure you I had no idea that was happening, and they did not have my support in this endeavor. I will punish them accordingly in my realm and they will not be allowed back."

I smile. "Even if you decided to let them come back, I have assured that would not be successful. They will not like the consequences of sneaking back through the passageway. They may have thought they were going unnoticed but I assure you we knew the whole time and were letting them lead us to where they would determine what they were trying to accomplish."

My dad is still glaring at the Faerie King. "Next time something like this happens I will not be so kind to only have them banished. They will remain in this realm and will suffer the punishment that we see fit. We are allowing you to prove you have control of your faeries and to prove to them that this kind of behavior will not be tolerated. If you fail and we have another problem of this magnitude, we will not give you that option again. The contract clearly states we may punish them in our realm for any wrong doing while here. They will not like the punishments we come up with."

The Faerie King nods his head. "I understand and agree. I will assure you, you will not have another problem from my faeries."

Dad sighs. "Now I think it would be a good idea for you to head back to your realm and deal with your faeries while we deal with the Troll King who will step out of that passageway in a few seconds."

The Faerie King turns and steps back to his realm as the Troll King steps through from his realm just as angry as the Faerie King had been.

Dad holds up his hands before the Troll King has a chance to say anything. Dad explains to him in as angry of a tone as he had to the Faerie King what had transpired.

When he is done, the Troll King is quicker with coming

up with his response and does not sputter at all. "I will support your decision to banish them and the spell placed on them if they try and reenter your realm. Even though our contract states they will be punished by their home realm I will uphold your punishment. I will also be punishing those for the embarrassment they have brought on their King and their realm."

He turns and steps back through the passageway.

CHAPTER 19

As they leave dad turns to me. "Close all the passageways for the rest of the day. I don't want anyone else coming through today."

I nod my head and do as he asks. He is on a rampage and I want to stay out of his way.

We watch as he paces and mutters to himself. He finally calms down and looks at us. He sighs. "I know I went a little overboard. I can't believe what those morons were having their faeries and trolls do. Then they have the nerve to come here and act like we are the ones doing something wrong. If it wasn't for the fact that I want to give the ones that don't agree with their rulers somewhere to go to get away from it I would close those passageways and not allow any of them here."

I'm not sure how dad will take the next thing I am about to say but I have to try and break the tension. "If it makes you feel any better, I'm pretty sure that at least a couple of them are going to try and come back through and see if they can ignore the pain. I think the faeries will think they have enough power to prevent it and the trolls will think they can handle the pain."

Dad laughs and hugs me. "Thanks honey I needed that. It will be pretty funny to watch as they realize they really can't come back here."

"Yeah, and then they will try to come here from another realm thinking they will be able to go around the spell. It should be pretty entertaining in the next day or so."

"That it will and we will be sure to keep an eye on it. I don't want anyone else to come through and try to take revenge for that spell."

I grin. "All that will accomplish will be them getting the same spell."

He smiles back at me. "That's my girl."

We all head back to the house early. I manage to pull Chase off to the side as everyone is going through the portal back to the house and I pull him through a different portal.

He smiles when he sees that I have brought him back to our beach. He pulls me close and places a soft sweet kiss on my lips. We turn to watch the beautiful sunset that is before us.

When the sun has once again fallen below the ocean we lay down on the sand to watch the stars emerge.

I sigh. "Look how big and beautiful the moon is tonight. It is so gorgeous here. I wish we had this kind of view at home."

He shifts so he can see my face. "I have the most beautiful view I could ever ask for every time I look at you."

I smile. "How did I get so lucky?"

"I am the lucky one."

We lay there and watch until all the stars have come out and then head back to the house to see what the others are up to.

When we step through the portal Penelope launches herself at me and I almost fall over from the force. I look at Chase with confusion as she hugs me so tight it is hard to breathe.

Landon is glaring at us and I have no idea what is going

on. I finally get Penelope to let go and I look at her worried face. "What is going on?"

Her jaw drops in shock. "What do you mean what's going on? You disappear as we are all coming back to the house and are gone without a trace for hours right after we had a huge fight with not one but two different realms. What happened? How was someone able to grab you and how did you get away?"

I look over at Chase with shock who is doing everything he can not to laugh at his sister. I glare at him when he loses the battle and starts laughing.

Penelope looks at him completely confused. "I don't see what's funny."

He calms his laughter down. "Relax drama queen. Nobody took us. Annisa and I went somewhere that we could have a little bit of alone time and relax. After the stress of the day Annisa needed to chill for a little bit."

Penelope goes from confused to pissed in a matter of seconds. She glares at us both. "Next time you two decide to sneak off you want to give us a little heads up. How are we supposed to know if you are in trouble if you take off and disappear like that?"

Rayne rolls her eyes. "By paying attention to the connection genius, that's how. If they had been in trouble they either would have opened up the connection and told us or their emotions would have been strong enough to grab our attention. If you had listened to me when I told you they were fine you wouldn't have shaved ten years off your life worrying about them."

She scowls. "Just because you said they were fine doesn't mean that they were. It could have been they were keeping their emotions in check to keep us safe and prevent us walking into a trap."

I laugh. "I promise if we are taken and are trying to keep you from walking into a trap I will open the connection and tell you it's a trap. We honestly didn't even think anyone would worry if we took a little detour on the way home."

She huffs out a breath. "I know you need some time to yourselves, Landon and I take that every chance we get it was just bad timing is all."

"I will keep that in mind for next time. Just remember you will be the first to know if we are in trouble and what is going on."

She nods her head and lets Landon lead her away. Landon is still glaring at us for making her worry like that.

I look over at Chase. "That was unexpected."

He laughs. "I told you she can be a drama queen."

I playfully smack his arm as we pick out a movie to sit down and watch. Rayne and Ethan have joined us and they are cuddled up on one of the couches while Chase and I cuddle up on another one.

It is a nice quiet relaxing night.

The next morning, we get to the clearing and open the passageways back up. We have a little catching up to do since the passageways were closed for so long yesterday.

Zenia came through first. "Is everything all right? I got worried when the passageways kept being closed yesterday. I want to make sure you are all right and it is ok to send elves through today."

I smile at her. "We had a little issue with the faeries and the trolls yesterday that had to be taken care of. We will do the best we can to get caught back up and get the ones that were scheduled yesterday and today where they are going."

We turn and look at the faerie that has appeared and is now laying on the ground screaming in pain. None of us move to help him and Zenia is watching it all with wide eyes. He crawls back to the passageway and manages to get himself back to his realm. I can hear Drake laughing on the other side.

"I told you she wouldn't be bluffing. Want to try again?"

We laugh as we hear the faerie say some words I'm not even sure I know what they mean.

Drake then sticks his head through smiling. "I had to let them see for themselves. Sorry about all the noise but that should let them know you were serious." He then ducks back into his realm.

Zenia is looking at us with wide eyes. I laugh. "Don't worry none of your elves have to worry about that. We had to banish a group of faeries and trolls and I put a spell on each of them that prevents them from entering our realm from any passageway without excruciating pain. We were expecting some of them to try and sneak back in. If any trolls or faeries come to your realm and try to come to this realm from there just let them. They will find they cannot evade the spell quick enough. Oh, and just a warning they will still be in pain if they try to go to any other realm besides their own after coming here. They must return to their home realm for the pain to subside."

She laughs. "How creative, today is going to be very entertaining. Do you mind if I keep the passageway open and watch?"

I smile at her. "Not at all, it is bound to be pretty entertaining."

We can hear that something is going on in her realm and she hurries back through the passageway to find out what is going on. We then hear her laugh and say, "Yes I know we don't usually allow beings from other realms to use our passageway to get to a different realm but today is different. Let him go."

We watch as a faerie steps through the passageway and smirks at us as he prepares to take off running. He doesn't even get one step before the smirk is gone and he is screaming in pain. He tries to go back through the passageway to the elfin realm and we can still hear his cries of pain. He returns to our realm and tries to glare at us through his pain as we watch him slowly make his way to the passageway back to his realm. We don't even attempt to help him reach the passageway. We just stand there and watch him struggle.

Drake had stepped through when he heard the screams and is leaning against a tree to the side of the passageway. He doesn't move to help his fellow faerie either.

Zenia steps back through and laughs as she takes in the scene of us watching the faerie try to get to the passageway to stop the pain.

As he makes it to the passageway and is trying to pull himself through it I say, "Tell the others exactly what happened here. We have no sympathy for you or the pain that you are causing yourself. We will not help in any way to alleviate your pain. We will stand by and watch you suffer as you stood by and watched the mortals suffer."

As he pulls himself through he glares at Drake. "Traitor. You could have helped me reach the passageway."

Drake grins. "King's Orders are that I may not assist you in any way. You are to find your way back on your own."

The faerie walks away defeated. Drake looks at us and smiles again. "I think I will leave the passageway open today so they are able to make it back. Plus, it looks to be an entertaining day in your realm today." He steps back through the passageway to his own realm again.

CHAPTER 20

Word must have spread quickly to the other faeries. There are only a few more attempts that day. They realized even if we are distracted by other faeries they will be stopped by the spell. They also find if two of them come through at the same time they will both be stopped and not just one of them.

As we watch the last of them making their way to the passageway while the one that was trying to distract us glares at us I roll my eyes. The faerie girl that had been flirting with Chase to distract us from the passageway reaches down to help her friend make it back to the passageway.

"I wouldn't do that if I were you," I warn her.

She glares at me and grabs a hold of her friend's arm. As soon as she touches him she drops his arm and writhes on the ground in pain. She glares at me through her pain as she makes her way back to the passageway.

Drake has been watching and starts to laugh. As she glares at him he reminds her, "I tried to tell you. Maybe now you will listen when I say you shouldn't do something. You will all learn you can't get away with the things you want to do in this realm."

He follows the two faeries back to his realm. I look around at the others. "I'm really surprised none of the trolls tried to come through today."

Landon smirks. "They will wait and see if we forget about them and try to sneak in while we are not paying attention. They think we have to activate the spell. They will figure out soon enough just them entering this realm is all it takes to activate the spell."

I let out an irritated breath. "Do they really think I would use a spell that would require our constant attention? Really, how realistic would that be and how would we ever be able to remember all the ones we banished?"

"That is what they are counting on. They are hoping if they give it a few days we will forget who all we banished and they might be able to sneak through."

I sigh. "Well, I guess we can't stop them from trying."

We have managed to get caught up even with all the faerie interruptions and close the passageways for the night. I look over at Penelope. "I promise nobody is taking me I just want to have a nice quiet dinner with my husband."

She laughs. "I promise I won't overreact anymore. You don't need to tell me every little move you are making. I think I learned more about your bathroom habits today than anything else."

I laugh. "Glad you figured out what I was doing."

We head back to the house to get ready for the evening plans we have. Chase and I have decided to go for a nice dinner and a movie. It is nice to have a nice normal date every once in a while.

Chase rolls his eyes as I tell the lady at the register we want two tickets to the latest romantic comedy that is playing. I laugh at him. "You lost fair and square. It's not my fault you always play the rock in rock, paper scissors. Since you always play rock, it means I always play paper. If you would mix it up just once you might actually win."

He laughs. "I did try mixing it up, and you figured out I was going to play scissors to beat your paper and you played rock. I can't win. We need to find a different way to make these decisions. I still think you peek in my mind to see what I am going to play so you know what to play."

I smile sweetly at him. "Now, that would be cheating. Are you accusing me of cheating?"

He laughs. "Oh, I would never accuse you of anything. I am flat out saying that you cheat."

I smack him playfully on the chest and he leans down and gives me a quick kiss before he orders the popcorn and sodas for the movie.

I love the movie and Chase even likes it, even though he would never admit it to anyone. We decide to head back to the house and see what everyone else is doing.

It isn't long after we get back when the others come home from their evening plans. We sit in the living room and the conversation moves toward what we are going to do about the faeries and the trolls.

Ethan has an idea. "We only banished the ones that we caught. You know there are smarter faeries and trolls that were not caught at the village. Some of them were smart enough to blend in with the mortals so they were not so easily found. It was only the most arrogant ones that we found. It is going to be harder to find and get rid of the rest of them. They are clever and know how to blend into this realm."

I sigh. "I have been thinking the same thing. We have only taken care of very few of the ones that are probably here. There will be more coming through and not acting in a way to draw attention to themselves. They will come in like they are genuinely interested in learning about our realm and try not to raise our suspicions."

Landon interjects "Those are the ones we need to be most worried about. The ones that are drawing attention to themselves or trying to sneak in are not clever enough to get away with anything. It's the ones smart enough to work the system that are going to accomplish something. That's why the Faerie King told Drake not to help the ones that were banished. If they were stupid enough to get caught, then they are worthless to him in his plan."

Penelope's snap open wide, shocked. "He is using our spell as a punishment for them getting caught? That is so cruel. How can a king treat his subjects like that? I really don't understand the way the faeries think."

Chase laughs. "Just because you think everyone should be treated fairly doesn't mean that is the way it's going to be everywhere. There are even mortal kings in our history that have treated their subjects like the Faerie King does. It is an abuse of power but one that will happen and we can do nothing about. We have no right to try and change the way they run their realms all we can do is dictate how everyone is treated while they are here in our realm."

Landon is thoughtful for a minute. "Now, we have to figure out who is here for the hybrids and who is here to learn about our realm. How are we supposed to figure out their reasons other than what they have said? They could easily take hybrids back with them if they have made friends with them and made the hybrids actually think they are wanted in the faerie and troll realms."

I think about that for a moment. "If the hybrids were raised away from the village, they are not going to have the same resentment to the other realms. The faeries and trolls that were smart enough to find a mortal and make a family instead of using the mortals as a breeding tool are going to have told the hybrids they had no way to get to their home realm. If the hybrids think that their faerie or troll parent was stuck here, and that is the only reason they were not allowed to go to that realm they will be excited to have the opportunity to go to the realm they have only heard about and probably dreamed about seeing one day. That is going to make it very hard to figure out who is doing this."

Penelope whips her head around. "You have the ability to sense them so you will know when a hybrid is brought to the passageways to be taken to another realm."

"Yeah, but if they truly want to go, we have no way to

prevent it. We have an agreement that allows anyone to travel to the other realms if they truly wish and have not been banned from that realm. I may know they are hybrids but that won't change anything. Plus, if a mortal got pregnant by a faerie or troll and there was no relationship there could be hybrids out there that know nothing of their heritage. It is possible there are hybrids out there the faeries and trolls know nothing about. Those hybrids are going to be drawn to the faeries and trolls feeling a connection with them they haven't ever felt with anyone else. Then when they are told about the other realms, they will be excited to explore."

Landon furrows his brow. "They will be able to sense the power in the hybrids. There are probably some that are here for that specific purpose. They will take the tours and keep their senses open to see if they can find any of the hybrids that have been created without the knowledge of the faerie or troll that created them. We all know that one night stands happen and sometimes the woman will get pregnant and with no way to contact the father or no desire to contact the father so the faerie or troll would have no idea there is a hybrid they created."

"I think we need to try and find some of the hybrids before the faeries and trolls do. I don't know how we should go about doing that. I think it needs to wait until this whole thing with the banishment calms down or they are going to know what we are doing. If Chase and I go to some of the places, we know the faeries and trolls are going and are only gone for a day at a time we might be able to track some of them down without the faeries and trolls figuring out what we are doing."

"That's a good idea but what are you going to tell the hybrids once you find them. Most of them are not going to believe you when you tell them about their missing parent. There are also probably faeries and trolls that have never told their mortal partner or any children about their heritage. If they don't tell them about it, then they are more likely to stay undiscovered. They could be biding their time until they are able to grab and take the hybrids back to their home realm. Most of the hybrids won't believe anything you tell them. The ones that know about it are going to have been taught from an early age to not let anyone know. Therefore, they are not going to admit to you if they do know and will think you are out to get them because you know about it and are trying to get them to confess to it."

"Yeah, that is going to make it harder. We will figure out what to say and what not to say. The problem is we don't know what will work and what won't and even when we find something just because it works for one doesn't mean it will work for any of the others."

"You are going to have to figure it out each time. You will not be able to go with a story all ready and just jump right into it. You will have to watch the hybrid and see what their situation is so you can find a way to break the news to them without raising their suspicion or them thinking you are some crazy person."

Chase sighs. "How exactly are we supposed to do that? We can't spend weeks watching each hybrid we find. We have to find them and talk to them all in one day."

I have an idea. "I think I have it figured out. We can find them and approach them. After we have made our initial contact, we will tell them about everything and then give them our phone number. We will tell them we know they probably don't believe us but we want them to be able to get a hold of us if they are approached by faeries or trolls. That way when we don't try and force them into anything and then the faeries and trolls come along and try to convince them they need to leave their home they will have someone to turn to. They will see we aren't trying to make them leave everything they know and everyone they love like the faeries and trolls are and that will give them at least a little bit of trust in us."

Landon smiles. "That is probably the best plan we can come up with. All we can do is give them the information and warn them about what is heading their way. Then they can choose for themselves what they want to do. Some of them will still want to go to the other realms and we can't do anything about that, but at least the ones that don't want to will know they have another option."

We talk about this for a while longer and then head up to bed. When we are in our room I look over at Chase. "I'm sorry I didn't talk to you first before I volunteered us to go off on our own again and look for the hybrids."

He smiles at me. "As long as you are including me in these little trips I am fine with it. I don't like it when you think you have to go off on your own without me."

I grin and we get ready for bed. I curl up against him in bed and am asleep not long after that.

CHAPTER 21

The next few days are pretty quiet. Only a couple more faeries try to come through. Word eventually got around they were all unsuccessful and no more try to come through.

We still haven't seen any of the trolls try and come through so we are thinking they are smart enough and have learned from the faeries that they will not be able to come through.

Just as Chase and I are starting to make plans on where we are going to go first to look for the hybrids our attention is diverted to the writhing and grunting troll on the edge of the woods.

I roll my eyes and look at him. "Well, I'm impressed you could make it as far as you did before you couldn't take it anymore. The problem with that is now you have further to go to get back to the passageway to get back to your realm."

Heath steps out of the passageway and glares at the troll on the ground. "Just because I stepped away from the passageway for a few minutes does not mean you can try and sneak through."

The only answer he gets is a grunt as the troll starts to try and crawl back to the passageway. Heath turns his back on the struggling troll. "All the trolls have been informed of what transpired and the banished ones have been instructed they are not to attempt to return to this realm. I apologize that this one slipped by us."

I smile. "You can't watch everyone all the time. It was only a matter of time before at least one of them tried to come through."

I roll my eyes as we hear another troll start to make the same grunting noises. I have to stifle my laughter as the troll stands with one foot in our realm and one in the troll realm. It looks like he thought if he came through slow enough he would be able to come in unnoticed. The problem is now half his body was in excruciating pain while the other half was fine.

I look around and see the others are trying not to laugh as well. "That must be a very strange feeling. Stopping in the middle never really crossed my mind. I can see what he was thinking but I can't imagine what it must feel like with half of me in that much pain and the rest fine."

Heath glares at the new arrival and he manages to pull himself fully back into the troll realm. The first troll has managed to get himself to the passageway and is pulling himself back to his home realm.

Heath glances back at us. "I hope they did not cause too much of an inconvenience for you."

I smile at him. "It's not a problem. We were actually surprised none of them had tried yet."

He gets a sinister looking smile on his face. "After those two are punished for defying a direct order from King Sebastian and the others hear of their fate when they got here I don't believe any of the others will attempt to reenter your realm."

He then turns and steps back to his own realm.

I look around at the others. "Am I the only one that thinks it's creepy how much they like to punish the trolls? Every time a punishment is mentioned the one doing the punishing gets a creepy smile while the one being punished looks terrified."

Chase gives me a sympathetic look. "Baby, it's not our problem to fix. How they deal with punishment in their realm is up to them. You don't want anyone coming here and telling us how we need to do things so you can't go there and tell them to change the way they have always done things. You have to accept that things are done differently in different realms and not interfere."

I nod my head with a sad look on my face as I watch the passageway to the troll realm. I am trying not to imagine what the King is going to do to the two trolls that had tried to come through but my imagination is running wild.

After a few minutes of gruesome visuals running through my head, I shake my head to try and clear it of the images.

The others have picked up the conversation where we had left off as if we hadn't been interrupted by the trolls.

Landon interjects, "I think you need to go to the areas that the faeries and the trolls have not had a lot of access to yet. That is the best chance you have of getting to the hybrids in those areas before they do."

I shake my head. "I think we should go to the areas where they have already been first. If they have already made contact with some of the hybrids, then those hybrids are going to be really confused and trying to figure out what they should do. If we go and let them know they don't have to change anything if they don't want to it will ease their tension and keep them from thinking they don't have a choice."

"Or you could be walking into a trap. The faeries and trolls could have told the hybrids anything they wanted about us. We have no idea what they think of us or if they have been told to immediately attack if they see us to protect themselves."

"That's exactly why we need to see them first. If the faeries and trolls have convinced them that they are in danger here in this realm they will be jumpy. They have no training on how to use their magick and it can easily backfire on them. If they are jumping at every little thing that could possibly be a danger to them then they will end up hurting an innocent bystander or themselves."

Everyone else has been listening to Landon and I debate the matter. I can tell none of them know which side they want to be on. Both sides make a good point. The problem is that Landon and I also know the other has brought up a good point.

I sigh. "Ok, we need to figure out which one would be better. I can see what you are saying and it goes along with what we were talking about with giving them the information and then when they were approached by the faeries and trolls they would not be so confused. I don't like the idea that there is possible ticking time bombs out there that will end up hurting someone if we don't do something."

Chase clears his throat. "I think they are both good ideas but why do we have to pick one? Can't we do both? One trip we could go to somewhere the faeries and trolls have had access to and the next go to one that they haven't. If we do it on an alternating basis, we will be able to take care of both sides."

I raise my eyebrows. "That's a good idea. That way we can try and prevent damage at the same time that we are trying to fix whatever damage has been caused."

Ethan furrows his brow. "You really think there is going to be damage to be fixed? I don't think they would do anything to draw attention to what they are doing."

"By the time the hybrids cause any damage there won't be any faeries or trolls there for us to blame the damage on. They are going to try and make the hybrids think they are not safe here. If the hybrids are causing damage the trolls and faeries will then be able to come to us and say the hybrids need to be in the realm they came from for their own protection and the protection of our realm. If they make us think the hybrids are dangerous to the mortals, then they will be able to take them to their realms with our help."

Landon sucks a breath in surprised. "That would make sense. They are going to tell the hybrids they are being hunted down and rounded up or even killed so then they will be paranoid and lash out when the one that came to them disappears. The fact that they move on will only support the claim they are making to the hybrids. They could even plant the seed saying if they suddenly disappear then they have been discovered trying to help the hybrids."

Chase looks worried about us walking into this kind of situation. "I'm not so sure this is a good idea. If they are going to be lashing out and trying to protect themselves, then we will be walking right into an ambush."

I smile. "All we have to do is put a protection shield around us and not fight back. Once they see we aren't fighting back, they will stop and see what is going on. If we are supposed to be trying to destroy them then why wouldn't we be attacking them as soon as we get there instead of just standing there? It will be the first crack in the story they were told."

He furrows his brow. "I still don't like it."

I roll my eyes at him. "I know, you don't like anything that has to do with anyone coming at me with magick. We will be fine we just have to get them to listen to us. Once they hear what we have to say and see we are truly leaving them alone after that then it will put enough doubt in their minds as to what the faeries and trolls told them."

"Of course, they could also think we are trying to trick them and lull them into a false sense of security. If they see the whole thing as a way that we are trying to manipulate them then no matter what we say or do it won't do any good."

"We have to at least try. They will play along even if they don't trust us just to get us to go away and to see what we will do. When they see that we don't come back and they are not bothered by any of us again it will show them we were serious. When the only ones that keep bothering them is the faeries and the trolls and they keep disappearing they will start to see they are being lied to."

Chase is still not sure about this plan but he nods his head anyway while nervously tapping his foot. He doesn't have a better idea, so he has no choice but to agree to this.

Ethan has been listening to all of this. "I think it is really important for us to get in touch with the hybrids. If they are the product of the more intelligent and cunning faeries and trolls, they will be smart enough to figure some things out on their own. They probably already know they are different just not how. They are wondering why and how they can do the things they can. You are all assuming they will believe whoever gets to them first. I think they are smart enough to listen to both sides and decide on their own. Some of them will react like you guys are saying but I think the majority of them will be suspicious of anyone that has knowledge of them or what they can do. They aren't going to blindly trust the first person who comes along and gives them something to grasp onto. In this day and age, they get online and research try to figure out if what they are being told is the truth or someone trying to scam them. That's the advantage we have. The faeries and trolls don't know all the resources available to the hybrids and that they don't have to rely on what they are told they can look things up and won't be as trusting the faeries and trolls think they will be."

Rayne adds, "They think they are better than everyone and that arrogance is going to show through. The hybrids are going be cautious of that. This realm is taught to question everyone and everything. The arrogance of the faeries and trolls will keep them from realizing that they hybrids are not groveling at their feet eating up everything they say."

I look at Chase and smile. He shakes his head at me.

CHAPTER 22

The next day while the others go to the passageways Chase and I go to the first location that the faeries had access to. We didn't give the host any warning we were coming. We didn't want the faeries and trolls to have any idea we would be there.

We step through the portal before the passageways are open so there is nobody there to greet us when we get there. We walk up to the cozy little bed-and-breakfast that serves as the shelter at this location.

We knock on the door and when the host answers it she is very polite. She has no idea who we are.

I smile. "Hi, I'm Annisa and this is my husband Chase."

She instantly becomes flustered as she recognizes our names. "I'm sorry I didn't know you were coming. I would have been at the portal to greet you if I had known!"

"We didn't expect you to be there to greet us. We had our reasons for not informing you of our arrival beforehand."

"I hope there isn't a problem. I have kept track of everyone like I am supposed to. I have all the ledgers if you want to see them. Nobody has been unaccounted for."

I smile to try and ease her mind. "You didn't do anything wrong. You are doing a great job. We have been getting your email updates right on time and everything looks great. We are here for other reasons that we really can't discuss."

She sighs in relief. "I understand there are parts of your duties that are not allowed to be discussed. Please come in and make yourselves at home. Let me know if there is anything I can do to help or if you need anything."

We follow her into the house. She was in the process of making breakfast and nobody had come down yet. We sit at the island so we can talk to her for a few minutes before we look around.

"We won't stay long. We just wanted to let you know that we are in the area. We want to be away from here before your guests start to come down for breakfast. We don't want them all to know we are here. They will recognize us from when they came into this realm."

"Is there a problem with one of my guests? I have not had any problems with any of them. They have all been very polite and have followed all the guidelines and rules without complaint. They all seem to really enjoy their time here."

I smile. "We are looking into something we would prefer the other realms not know about yet. There is no problem and we are not here for anybody."

"Ok, well are you sure you don't want some breakfast before you go?"

"We already ate, but thank you for the offer."

We say our goodbyes and start to walk away from the cozy little house. I look over at Chase as we are walking. "It really is beautiful here. At least we will get to see some nice places while we are doing this."

He smiles at me. "I wish we were here for a vacation and not walking into a potentially very dangerous situation."

I laugh. "You worry way too much. We will be fine."

We walk into the little town that is not far from the bed-and-breakfast. It is still a little early for most people to be out and about. Some of the shops are open this early so we decide to play like tourists and start walking through some of the shops and looking around. We aren't really shopping but we make it look like that is our real purpose here.

While we are making our way through all the little shops, I keep my senses open to try and feel out any magickal beings. We sit down at a cozy little café for lunch before I finally feel something out of the ordinary.

As soon as she walks in, I can feel it. I look up quickly. Chase raises his eyebrows in question and I nod my head slightly to let him know we have found one hybrid. I am trying really hard not to stare but I want to make sure I keep my eye on her so she isn't able to sneak out and we lose her.

She senses me watching her and looks around to see who it is that has triggered that feeling. I am lucky in that she is sitting behind Chase so I am able to look at him and still see her in my periphery. She can only see me looking at Chase and won't realize I am the one watching her, I hope.

We finish our lunch and pay the bill. She is still eating when we leave. We retreat around the corner so we can watch the entrance to the café and follow here when she comes out.

It takes her another 15 minutes to come out of the café. We are able to stay a little bit back from her and stop every once in a while, to look into a window to try to keep her from noticing us.

It isn't until I realize she is leading us through side streets in a zig zag pattern that I know she is aware are back here and is waiting to see how long it will take us to make our move.

I look over at Chase and he nods his head slightly to let me know he has realized the same thing. Suddenly she stops, spins on her feet, and faces us with her hands on her hips and a scowl on her face.

"Alright, I know you want something so stop following me around and spit it out."

I look at her shocked. "You aren't even nervous we have been following you or not knowing what it is we want?"

"I have been expecting you. I suppose I should take you to the house so we can all sit down and talk and get it all over with. Follow me."

She spins around on her heel again and continues to walk. We don't go in a zig zag pattern anymore she leads us in a direct path to a house a couple of blocks away.

I look up at Chase and see the same stressed and worried expression on his face that he had last night when he realized this could be a potentially dangerous mission.

We get to a beautiful old Victorian style house and follow the girl in. She is probably about 19 or 20 years old and beautiful. She calls out when we step inside. "Mom, Dad, you need to come down here."

We see a couple come down the stairs with questioning looks on their faces. When they see us, understanding instantly takes over. They sigh and led us into a sitting room.

After we are all seated the faerie man looks over at his nervous mortal wife and then back to us. "I knew this was coming, but I was hoping to have a little more time for us to be a normal family."

I look at him confused. "Why would us being here stop you from being a normal family?"

"Now that both you and the faeries know about Chastity you will both be trying to recruit her for your side. I know how valuable the hybrids are and how powerful they are."

The girl glares at her father. "If you had told me about this sooner, it wouldn't have been a problem. I would have known to stay away from that asshole faerie when he approached me. He's lucky I didn't know anything, so I was thrown off a little bit about what he was saying."

The man sighs. "Chastity, I told you I didn't think they would ever find us so there was no reason to make you paranoid about anyone coming and taking you away."

I interrupt them. "We didn't come here to take your daughter or to recruit her. We only came to make sure you know the whole story and are not tricked by the faeries. We have no intention of doing anything or fighting the faeries."

He smiles a sad smile at me. "Then you will lose. They are working on putting an army together and if you will sit by and not prepare you will have no chance of winning this war. I admit I was hoping to keep my daughter out of all of this, but I was raised in the faerie realm. I was brought over here when I was about my daughter's age. I know exactly what they are doing. It was always the plan to find the hybrids when the realms were open so they could be used to take over all the other realms. They have been planning this for generations."

I smile. "Well, since the village turned against them and the ones that were being trained to fight for them have refused that will be very difficult for them. The strength they were counting on has decided they will fight for their mortal parents and not their faerie or troll ones."

His head snaps up at this revelation. "The village turned against them? That can't be. Those kids were bred with the sole purpose of being warriors. They were trained from birth. Their whole belief system was founded on them not being welcomed here but being trapped here with no access to their true realm."

"That only works if they don't treat the loving parent of the child so badly. The children resented the faeries and trolls for the way their mortal parents were treated. The mortals were the only ones that cared about the children and what they needed. They were cared for by the mortals and trained like dogs by the faeries and the trolls. The faeries and trolls that were in the village have been banished and are unable to reenter this realm."

He laughs. "They will sneak in as they have done in the past and then they will sneak the children back into their realm."

"That is not possible. I have put a spell on each of the banished ones that creates excruciating pain as soon as they enter this realm. The only way to end the pain is to return to their home realm. It doesn't matter which realm or passageway they try to come through. The spell is on the person and it will be triggered by their entrance to this realm."

He starts laughing. "I bet they are not too happy with you

right now."

I grin. "No, they aren't. Since they were caught trying to force children to their realm, the King has no option but to uphold this restriction. I am assuming you have already been approached by faeries that have given you a story about how we are going to come in here and force you and your daughter to go with us?"

He nods his head. "I knew that was not the case. I knew you would not force us to go, but I did think you would come here and keep coming back until we finally agreed. I know how important it is to protect your realm from the faeries. If their magick was brought here, it would be very difficult for this realm to fight back against something they know nothing about."

"We have no intention of coming back. We only wanted to forewarn you they would be coming. We also wanted to let you know about the system we have for the other realms to travel and learn about our realm. The faeries that come here and say if they disappear it will be because we found them and something happened to them is not true. They are scheduled to be at each place for a specified amount of time. In an attempt to keep us from discovering what they are doing they are following the rules and guidelines and moving onto the next location when scheduled. That is why they disappear they are simply following a schedule."

He furrows his brow as he processes this new information. "I thought that sounded a little off. I wondered why three of them have made contact and then disappeared and you still had not come to us. I thought if what they were saying was true then you would have come to us after the first one. If you had found him and taken care of him for informing us, then you would know about us and would be on our doorstep. The longer we went without hearing from you the more their story didn't make sense."

"We have not done anything nor do we intend to do anything to any faerie or hybrid. You have just as much right to live your lives as you see fit as we do. If you wish to join with us, we will not turn you away, but we will not actively try to recruit you."

"It is best for my family if we don't get involved. We would like to continue on as we always have. I feel this realm is my home here and I refuse to put my daughter in the position to get hurt in this matter. It is not by her choice that she is half faerie. If she wishes to learn how to use her magick, then I will teach her and she will do so in a manner to not be discovered by the mortals."

I smile. "I understand completely. Here is my phone number and email address. If you need anything, please feel free to contact me at any time. I will see what I can do to help you if you need it."

He takes the card I hand him and puts it in his wallet. He then leads us to the door. As we are leaving, he leans down and says quietly so his wife and daughter would not here him. "They won't give up that easily. You will have a fight. I don't want my daughter involved but I will help you if you need it. As long as my daughter is left out of it all I will do anything that is needed to protect her and her way of life here with her mother."

I nod my head and we start our walk back to the portal.

CHAPTER 23

We step back through the portal and let everyone else know how it went. We explain about the faerie and his daughter and the offer that was made.

Landon looks thoughtful for a minute. "Why would he think we would need that help? Without the hybrids from the village, they don't have a chance and would be stupid to start something."

I sigh. "He said they have been planning this and working toward it for generations. They will not give up that easily. If they have been counting on this to be the chance, they need to finally take control they aren't going to accept that it won't work and give up simply because one part of it didn't work out the way they wanted."

"Yeah, but that was the most important and crucial part of their plan. Without the hybrids that have been trained for this for their entire lives they have lost half their army. Surely they won't still try and take control of the realms without that backup."

"I think they are counting on the village hybrids to change their minds when the time comes. They think when it comes down to time to fight those hybrids won't be able to fight against their own parents, the ones that raised them and trained them. They don't realize how deep that resentment goes. They also don't see how much they hurt those kids by treating the mortal parent so badly. They can see how their parents were treated so why would they think they would be treated any differently if they joined forces with the faeries and trolls."

Ethan joins the conversation. "I think we will see them try something but I don't think it will work. I think they are going to send other faeries here to try and convince the hybrids to come back to the other realm. Or they may force them back, but the training they gave the hybrids will work against them. The hybrids are trained to fight and win they can use those skills to protect themselves and their mortal parents."

Penelope interjects, "I think it doesn't matter if they get the hybrids to help them or not. They will still try and take control. They think the hybrids will give them more of an advantage but they think they are smart enough and strong enough to win without the hybrids. They also know the hybrids' weaknesses. They are the ones that trained them so they know where to strike to cause the most damage. They are going to know how to manipulate the hybrids to try and get what they want. We have to watch for hybrids that are being forced not by sheer force but also by mental manipulations."

"It wouldn't take much. All they would have to do is kidnap the mortal parent and then hold them hostage to get the hybrid to do what they are told. It would be the most effective way to control the hybrids by using the one person they are trying to protect."

I smile. "I don't think the hybrids will be that easy to control. I can tell by the way they acted when we sent all the faeries and trolls from the village back to their realms. I think the hybrids would attack the ones that kidnapped their mortal parents and try and get them back instead of rolling over and doing what they are told. They have been trained their whole lives to fight and manipulate they don't know how to sit down and be taken advantage of."

Penelope asks, "Do you think we should track some of them down and let them know what we think is going to happen? Maybe we should try to protect them somehow. If we were there to help, then the mortal parents wouldn't be in so much danger."

I laugh. "I think we would be in the way. Remember the mortal parents have been around this for a very long time. They know what to expect and where to watch for danger. I'm sure they already know the faeries and trolls will come for them. The faeries and trolls are in for a surprise when they find the mortal parents are not as weak and helpless as they think they are. They knew they couldn't win in the village being that outnumbered but when it comes down to this, they will only be faced with a few. They won't sit by and bide their time anymore but will fight back and will have the hybrids to help. I think they will be fine and we need to stay out of the way on that one. We have let them know to contact us if they need our help so if they call then we will go if not we will let them handle the situation in whatever way they see fit."

We don't want to let on to the faeries and trolls what is going on so Chase and I don't make another trip until the next week. While we are monitoring the passageways for that week everything is quiet and moves along smoothly. I am starting to wonder what is going on.

"It's been a week with nothing out of the ordinary going on. I am getting a little nervous."

Landon laughs. "Well, since we are taking things slower

to make sure they don't figure out what we are doing, you should have already figured it out they are doing the same thing. They don't want us to know what they are up to anymore than we want them to know what we are up to. They have found when they do things right away we are expecting them. They want us to think they have given up so they are biding their time. They are still doing what they have been they are trying to do it where we don't see it."

"I'm sure you're right, but I still don't like it."

Chase comes up behind me and wraps his arms around my waist. "Baby, everything is fine. Don't let them get to you—that's what they want. You have to remember they are patient and can wait for what they want. They have been working up to this for generations and don't want to blow it by being impatient. They are going to wait and watch for the best time to act."

I pout. "Ok, I see your point. We really should get going. It should be safe to go through the portal without being seen now. Everyone at this location should have already left for the day to go about their plans."

He nods his head and grabs my hand. When we are on the other side we stop and admire the view for a minute before we head into the small town that is not far away.

When we get to the town, I instantly fall in love with it. "Chase, look it looks like Santa's Village. It is so quaint and quiet. I almost hate to disturb it."

He smiles. "It really is beautiful here. I hope we can keep anything from disturbing the peacefulness here."

We walk around and admire the little village. We do some window shopping and walk hand in hand enjoying the feeling of walking around like a normal couple on a little getaway.

We are looking in the window of a cute little boutique when I feel it. There is a hybrid standing behind us. I focus on the reflection in the glass instead of trying to look through it. As soon as I do, I made eye contact with the very tall and built teenager standing behind us with a scowl on his face.

Chase had felt me stiffen when I sensed the hybrid and

had focused on the reflection in enough time to see the boy indicate he wants us to follow him. Chase looks down at me with a worried expression.

I shrug my shoulders and follow the boy to see where he will lead us.

With how tall and big he is the boy has to be half troll. I hope he was not raised in the same way the trolls were in their realm or we could be walking into a situation Chase is really not going to like.

We come to a little cottage that sits back a little bit from the road. We follow the boy inside and wait just inside the door where he indicates.

A couple of minutes later a very tall woman and a smaller man come into the hallway smiling. The woman laughs. "Sorry, you know how moody teenagers can be. As soon as we felt you in the village, we sent him out to bring you back here. Apparently to a teenager that is the same thing as treating him like a dog and telling him to fetch. Please come in and have a seat."

I look up at Chase and he still has a worried expression. I tug on his arm to get him to follow me into the living room to sit and talk to the couple.

As soon as we are seated Chase asks, "What do you mean as soon as you felt us in town?"

She smiles. "I have a talent for sensing other magickal creatures. I have trained myself to be alerted whenever another magickal creature has entered this town, which has been quite often lately. I can also tell what type of creature they are and how powerful they are."

Chase shifts nervously in his seat. "So, do you have your son lead them all to your home to question them when they get here?"

She smiles at me. "He is very protective, isn't he?"

I laugh and nod my head while Chase scowls at us both.

She chooses to ignore his scowl and answers his question. "Most of the time I tell my son to be careful and to avoid any new people in town. He knows if I tell him to avoid someone there is a reason, and he actually does it. He can be sneaky and will usually watch them without them being aware just to see what they are doing and try to figure out why I told him to avoid them. I recently told him about his troll heritage which is what his foul mood is about. He didn't like that I kept it from him for so long. He also has this whole notion about how trolls have been described in this realm. I tried to explain the whole thing to him but I think he only listened to part of what I was saying."

The man next to her starts to laugh. "He is upset he can't tell anyone about it."

She smiles. "He thought it was great until I got to the part where he can't tell anyone about any of this. Anyway, I have kept him hidden from any of the trolls that have found their way here. They don't know he is here, and I have explained to him how important it is that they not discover him. I know the realms are open that is the only way that so many of them could make their way here. This is our home, and he knows very little about the troll realm. I want to keep it that way. I don't want him to ever have to witness or just stand by and watch as someone he loves is tortured in the name of punishment. The trolls are cruel and I don't want him exposed to that."

I nod my head to show I understand. "Even with your precautions there is still the chance he could approach one of the trolls and seek more information. If he were to show himself to them, they will have many reasons he needs to go to the troll realm with them and how we are only going to use him for our own needs."

She let out a frustrated breath. "I actually offered to go and find one of the trolls when the next one came through. He looked at me like I was crazy. I have already explained to him that if he wants to go there I would contact his grandparents and he could stay with them but I would never step foot in that realm again and that his father would not be welcome there. He has no interest in going to a realm I feel so much hatred toward that I refuse to even step foot in there and would not allow his father as an equal part of our family."

I smile. "Why did you send him to get us if you had already worked out a way to keep him hidden and he has no desire to be found by the other trolls?"

"I didn't want you to continue to come back and lead the trolls to us. If you kept coming back here, they would know there was a hybrid here you are looking for. If I just told you about all of this, then you could move on and we could continue to shield him."

"I understand and you will not see us again. We will not tell anyone other than the other Guardians here in our realm that we found you. I want to let you know the village has been destroyed and the faeries and trolls that were there have been banished and unable to return to this realm. We have placed a spell on each of them to prevent them from returning. The hybrids that were in that village turned on their faerie and troll parents and protected their mortal parents. They were not willing to harm their mortal parents and resented them for the harm they caused."

She grins. "I'm glad to hear those children are finally able to have a normal life. I always felt so bad for them but didn't have any way to help them."

"Thank you for explaining what you are doing. We will go now and leave you to live out your lives as you see fit. Here is my card please contact me if you ever need anything or there is anything I can do to help."

She puts my card in her purse and walks us to the door. The sullen teenager is nowhere to be seen.

As we are walking into town, I can feel the hybrid hiding. I stop and approach the little alleyway where he is sitting.

He smiles. "I knew you could sense me. I could tell by the way you looked at me in the window. My mom thinks I don't know what all is going on. I know more than she gives me credit for. I have known for a while now what I am. They would discuss it at night when they thought I was asleep on when was the best time to tell me. I think they would have put it off a lot longer if the trolls hadn't showed up here and she was afraid I would be too curious about them. I also heard her telling my dad about the things she had seen and gone through growing up in the troll realm. I never want to go there. If her parents will do that to her then I don't want anything to do with them. I wanted to let you know that I know not to approach them and to keep myself hidden. I realized a long time ago that I am more powerful than my mom. I know that's why they want me."

I smile a sad smile. "You know so much more than your mom wants you to. I'm glad you understand the whole situation. Here is my card if you ever find yourself in trouble and need help call me. I can create a portal to where you are and be there in seconds."

He nods and puts my card in his wallet.

CHAPTER 24

The next week goes by quickly. It isn't long before Chase and I find ourselves going through another portal to another beautiful location.

I look around at the scenery. "We really gave them beautiful places to visit, didn't we? I wish we could visit these places on an actual vacation instead of coming here on missions."

He laughs. "Someday we will be able to take vacations. Right now, we have to concentrate on the faeries and trolls and keeping them from starting a war that will do a lot of damage to our realm."

I sigh. "I know. I hope that once we show them, this won't work they will learn to stay in their own realm and leave the others alone."

He smiles at me. "Always the optimist."

As we have been talking we have been walking into the small town. I love that we have set all the shelters outside of small towns. It makes it more comfortable to come to the locations. It would have been easier for the other realms to blend in if it had been big cities but it would have been too much on their senses to be thrown into a big city. They were not used to our realm or our technologies and it was too much to take in all at once.

We are using the same technique that we have used in the other towns and act like tourists looking at all the shops when I feel the hybrids approaching us. I can also sense they will not be as friendly as the others. I look up at Chase with a worried look.

He looks back at me with a confused look that gets worse when I shake my head slightly to let him know I can't explain right now.

Just then I feel the magick wrap around the protection shield I had put up. They don't realize we have the shield and think they have us snared in their magickal rope. I can feel what they are trying to have the magick make us do so I turn us in the direction they are trying to make us go so they won't notice they don't have the control they think they do.

It doesn't take long for Chase to figure out what is going on. He can feel what they are trying to do against the shield too. Understanding flashes in his eyes when he realizes I haven't had time to warn him with more than my look that they were near and that their intentions were not friendly. He then glares at the group of hybrids standing before us with smug smirks on their faces.

The faerie hybrid that is standing in front of the others seems to be the leader. He has a self-satisfied smile on his face. "I am the strongest so don't even try to struggle you won't be able to break free. Even my dad can't get free from my binding."

It takes everything I have to not laugh and show him he really doesn't have us bound at all. Instead I continue to look at him as he continues.

"I thought you would at least have something to say about being taken by surprise and bound. Oh well, it doesn't matter. Just come with us if you struggle it will only draw attention and since we are not allowed to expose our magick it will be you and not us that gets punished."

I nod my head to indicate I understand. In reality I am

afraid to say anything because his attitude is pissing me off. I am afraid if I start talking I will keep going until I have told him more than he needs to know.

We follow them for a couple of blocks and are led to a decent sized house with many cars parked in the driveway and out front. It looks like some kind of party or meeting is happening here. The leader of this little gang has a very satisfied smile on his face as he leads us into a living room with a group of faeries and trolls all sitting around discussing something.

When we walk in they all stop talking and stare at us with open mouths. A faerie that looks a lot like the leader of our little gang stands up and faces the children with a look of pure fury.

I cringe as he starts in on his son. "What the hell were you thinking?!"

The boy loses his smile and stammers, "I…we…um…we caught them for you."

"You are 13 years old and have tried to bind two of the Guardians of the Passageways in this realm? Do you really think your binding is doing anything to them?"

"We bound them and brought them here. Of course, it is working on them. Even you can't break free from my bindings. They could feel the power and didn't even try to fight…" with that realization dawned in his eyes as his voice trails off.

"Of course, they didn't fight you. You were leading them to where they wanted to go. You are the ones they were looking for. They had no reason to fight you when you were giving them exactly what they wanted."

The boy looks over at us with wide eyes. I shrug my shoulders and walk into the room from the hallway with Chase right behind me. He watches with his jaw dropping onto his chest.

"Dad, I swear they could not move. I had them completely bound they couldn't even talk!"

The father pinches his nose between his eyes as he takes a

deep breath so he can calm down and explain to his son what happens when you get overconfident.

"Ok, we wanted to talk to them and we would have brought them here anyway so you have done no damage. What you need to realize is they were never bound by you. They had cast a protection shield that was undetectable to you but let them know exactly what you were trying to get them to do. They could do what you were forcing them to do to make you think your binding was working. Yes, your binding is strong enough for faeries and trolls but not for Guardians."

He looks over at us again shocked. I again shrug my shoulders and give him a sympathetic look. "Sorry, kid but your dad's right. I felt you coming and knew exactly what you planned to do. Since this was the first time we saw a group of hybrids together since the village we wanted to see what was going on so we played along."

The rest of the kids all look ashamed for what they have done but the leader of the little group is getting angry he had been played. "You are just like that faerie said you would be!"

"WHAT?!?!" the father bellows.

The kid cringes at his father's tone. "He told me not to tell you because you would take me to them and they would make me do things to other faeries. They made him disappear. He was coming and telling me all about the war they tried to take over all the realms and they were finding hybrids and forcing them to fight for us and kill our own kind."

The father looks like he is ready to smack his son upside the head. He restrains and takes another deep breath to calm down before he speaks to his son again. "Did it ever occur to you he was lying to you? I have never given you any reason to believe that is something I would do. I have also told you how the faeries are manipulative and will do anything to get their way and are always looking for more power."

The son looks confused and doesn't know what to believe. "Then why did he disappear? They had to do something to him to keep him from coming back."

I sigh. "We didn't do anything to him. We have a system for the other realms to come and visit this realm. It is like a scheduled tour. They are scheduled at each place for about two weeks and then they move onto the next location."

The father interrupts. "Which you would have known if you had bothered to come to me with this since I already knew about it and could have told you. After the mess with the village they are doing everything they can to not bring attention to themselves."

I look at him with surprise. "You seem to know a lot about what is going on."

He sighs. "There is a reason we are meeting. We felt you arrive, and we were discussing the best way to approach you. If my son had bothered to actually listen to what was going on, he would have known we were not looking for you to attack you but so we could tell you what we have learned."

He gives his son a glare, and he finally looks ashamed for his actions. "Do you want us to go back outside now?"

The father sighs again. "No, you need to hear this. Everyone take a seat we have a lot to discuss."

Chase and I sit on empty chairs and the kids all sit on the floor. They are still in a group and they are avoiding making eye contact with their parents who are all glaring at their kids.

When we are all seated, the faerie that seems to be the leader of the adult group looks at us with a look I can't decipher. "I still have contacts with people at the village. All of our children were born there. We took them away when they were still infants. We could get away in the middle of the night as a group with our mortal spouses. It wasn't easy, but it was needed. When the village was taken down and the faeries and trolls sent back a couple of the mortals contacted us. We had always been kind to them and they wanted to know if they could join us here. I had to tell them no because I didn't want to draw more faeries and trolls here by them coming here. It was hard enough for our group to stay hidden with how many of us are here. Bringing in more would make it impossible."

I look around and see the guilty look that all the adults wear. Then I look down at the kids and see the confusion there. "They don't know any of this, do they?"

"No. We saw no need to tell them what was happening in the village. There was nothing we could do about it so there was no need to burden them with it. They have been raised in this realm like any mortal child. The only difference is after they get home from their mortal school they have another class here where we teach them to control their magick. We want to make sure they know how to control it so there is never an accident when they get angry so we have been teaching them from the time they could understand what was happening. To them magick is part of who they are. It is ingrained in them and they have complete control. It was the best solution we could come up with to keep them from accidentally exposing us all."

I nod my head. "That makes sense and is a very good idea. I don't understand why you needed to meet with us to explain that."

"That's not what we needed to meet with you about. That is so you understand how we live. We want you to know we have taught them what they need to know to blend in with this realm and they are not a danger to any of us by exposing magick. We know what the faeries and trolls are planning and how they plan to do it. We were all placed in the position to be taken to this realm when the passageways would take someone. We had researched and watched and found the area and the time that each was taken. That way we knew exactly where to place someone to be sent here. That gave us the ability to place who we wanted here to be ready when the passageways were open. We were all a part of that and even participated in the planning of what this would accomplish."

"I don't understand. If you were all part of the plan why did you leave the village?"

"We love our kids and our spouses and we can't do to them what is planned. When we realized that we loved them we couldn't put them in the position that would destroy not just them but also this realm and possibly all the realms."

The son looks at his dad and rolls his eyes. "Really, dad, you expect us to believe you helped to plan something that would destroy all the realms and kill people?"

He sighs. "If only it was that simple. It is actually so much worse."

CHAPTER 25

I look at him and wait for him to explain. The son stares at his father with his jaw on his chest. He was not expecting that kind of answer. The tone of voice the man had used made it perfectly clear to us all that he was completely serious.

He looks around at us all and the other adults give him nods of encouragement. He sighs and continues. "The Faerie King doesn't want to just take control of the other realms he wants to enslave them. He thinks the faeries are so much better than everyone else and they should all be working for us and doing our bidding. The trolls don't realize they are not exempt from this. They think since they are helping to get the power needed to win they will be equal partners with the faeries. They are actually looking forward to being able to torture other realms instead of just the trolls. The Faerie King plans to use them as enforcers to make everyone do what he wants but he will never give them any real power. By the time the trolls realize this it will be too late to do anything. They will have alienated themselves from all the other realms and will have nobody to help them. It is a very thought out plan that has been in the works for generations."

I look at him confused. "We already know all of this. That's why we worked so hard to make sure they didn't get the power they needed."

He gives me a sympathetic look. "He already has it. All he is looking for in the hybrids is the added bonus to be able to take over and enslave the realms quicker."

I am still confused. "What could he possibly have that would give him that power?"

"He has control of the Origin of all Magick. That is why the faeries think they are better and stronger and deserve to be worshiped. The Origin is in the faerie realm."

While the adult faeries look defeated and the hybrid children look shocked I look over at Chase and we both smile.

The man stares at us confused. "What could you possibly be smiling about?"

"He may think he has control of the Origin but I can assure you he doesn't."

"I have seen it and I have felt the power. I would not have agreed to what I did if I was not entirely sure of the fact there was no way to win against him. He can draw power from the Origin and that will give him the power he needs to be successful."

I shake my head. "Come with me and I will show you something."

He stands and I walk outside. I create a portal to a place of power in an area that is nowhere close to where the true Origin is. As soon as we step through the portal, the man looks around in wonder.

"He has the control of a place of power not the Origin. There are many places of power like this in this realm. Since magick is not used freely here, there are different spots that the magick congregates. It has to have somewhere to go when it is not being used regularly."

We step back through the portal to his house. He walks in with a shell-shocked look on his face and the other adults stand up ready to defend him. He waives his hand to indicate to them to sit back down.

"How is this possible? There is more power in that one spot then I have ever felt before. There is more there then even the Faerie King has control over. Is that the true Origin?"

I shake my head. "No, that is not the true Origin and I won't tell you where that is. We know where it is and we have control of it but there are very few of us that know the true location. Those places of power are only there because magick is not being used and is therefore building up in those locations. I think what happened is that your King happened across an area that was not populated in your realm and the magick had built up and since he had never experienced that before he thought he had stumbled onto the Origin."

The man finally smiles. "That means he will attack thinking he has no chance of losing when in reality he has no chance of winning."

I put my hand up to stop him. "We will not get overconfident with this. Even though we have control of the Origin and can draw on its power does not mean we will win. There are many factors that will play into that."

He nods his head. "Of course, I reverted to my old way of thinking in my excitement. I agree you are correct in it will depend on how the war is fought. I fear that this realm will still suffer a great deal of damage during a war between the realms."

I sigh. "I am hoping to take the war to another realm. The mortals here can't handle knowing about magick. I mean, look at the Salem Witch Trials. We have to try and keep this from them for our safety and theirs. I plan to take it to the faerie realm. I think it is only fair since they are the ones starting this war it should be their realm that suffers the damage of it."

He laughs. "I think I like the way you think. You seem like the type to give out a punishment and not feel bad about someone getting what they deserve."

I sigh again. "As long as they deserve it I am fine with it. It's when they don't deserve the punishment that they are made to suffer that I have a problem. I don't like that any realm will suffer damages from this. The faeries that don't agree with the King will have to deal with the damage too and that is really not fair to them. The problem is I can't let this realm suffer the damage since most of the people here have no idea there are even more realms let alone that we are at war with one."

"We can be very helpful to you in this. We would prefer that our children not be involved, but they have been trained and are skilled. They will also try and sneak in when we are not looking so it is better if we let them participate and know exactly where they are and what they are doing. They are less likely to get hurt if they are not trying to keep us from seeing them."

I laugh. "I think that sounds like a great idea. We don't want to let the faeries or trolls know what is going on or that we know what they are attempting. While we are still trying to get everything situated just go about your lives like you normally would."

He nods and then looks over at his son. "If you are approached by anymore faeries or if any of you are approached by faeries or trolls, you act like they are convincing you of their story. You pretend that you know nothing and that they are giving you information that you believe."

They all smile at each other and the man sighs. "Yes, I know how convincing you can all be when you put your minds to it. Just use those skills to help us keep them from knowing we are turning the tables on them. This will also give you all the opportunity to see the realms where we are from. I want you to understand though that when this is over we will be coming back here and will continue on with our lives like this never happened. We will never move to another realm. When you are adults, we will tell you everything about our realms so you can decide for yourself if you want to go and live there or stay here."

The troll hybrids shudder at the thought of living in the troll realm. The man narrows his eyes at the troll adults.

They all look sheepish and one man answers the unasked question, "We wanted them to understand what our kind was like. We didn't know if they would start to have urges towards cruelty since they were not raised around it. We wanted them to come to us if they felt anything like that. We had to explain to them why we were asking. It looks like all we have done is put a bad image of our realm in their minds. Which we were fine with because we never want them to endure what we did in that god-awful place and this was the best way to give them the information before they learned about it by experiencing it."

The man nods. "I see your problem. I'm glad to hear that the cruelty is something that is taught and not genetic. I don't blame you for making sure they know exactly what they would be walking into if they went to your realm. Just from some of your stories I had nightmares."

"After living through it the nightmares were horrible. I hate that when we came here, I kept expecting horrible things to happen and was always watching to make sure that nothing happened to the kids. Even after all these years I am still watching over my shoulder."

I give him a sympathetic look. "I can only imagine what you have lived through and endured. We have only seen the terrified look in the eyes of the troll heading to the King to hear his punishment and the anticipation in the eyes of the one that will get to perform that punishment. Just the terror in their eyes was enough to make me lose sleep. I know I can't interfere and that is how things are done in that realm but I want to leave the option open for the ones that don't agree with it to escape here to this realm."

He nods his head. "I appreciate that. I am sure there are some in my family that are preparing to come here if they can escape. They are most likely waiting to see the outcome of the war. They will not risk throwing their hat in with the other side if there is a chance they will lose. They will not risk the punishment that will bring."

Chase gives him a sad smile. "I don't blame them. I think I would sit back and wait and see what happens too. With something like that hanging over your head you have to think about your family and what is best for them. We won't hold it against them. We don't plan on holding any grudges after this is over. Once the Faerie King and the Troll King are put in their place and they know their plan won't work, we will continue to leave the passageways open and welcome all to this realm."

I add, "We know there will still be some that will continue to try and find some way to beat us. We also know we are going to have to ban some from this realm. We will not do that lightly. We don't want to ban someone that was being forced to do something. We will check out each person and their circumstances before we ban them. It was easier with the village because the children were the ones that decided on who was worth having and who needed to be sent back. Unfortunately, the only ones still there all should be sent back. It freed the children and the mortals and protected them from their tormentors so it was a good thing. I don't want to banish people until we know for sure they need to be banished."

They look at me with shock. The faerie man that is the spokesperson for the group asks, "You are actually worried about the people in our realms?"

I furrow my brow at him. "Why wouldn't I be?"

"Because all the realms take care of their own and don't bother themselves with the problems of the other realms. You are the first person that is actually trying to help the other realms."

I sigh. "I hope to change that. I hope once this is all over all the realms will be able to work together and we can all live in the realm we want to without worry about whether or not we are welcome. I don't think that it needs to be so separated. If you are not happy where you are then you should have the option to move to somewhere you could be happy."

He looks over at Chase with his eyebrows raised.

Chase laughs. "Yeah, I know she is so optimistic. She refuses to believe that it might not work out that way. Good thing is she has always gotten her way, and she doesn't know how to give up until she gets what she wants."

I glare at him. "We really need to be getting back before someone notices we have been gone for too long."

We talk for a couple of more minutes and then head back through town to take the portal back to the Origin.

CHAPTER 26

We don't need to make any more trips to visit any hybrids. The word has traveled fast and we are getting emails and calls from the faeries and trolls that had taken refuge in our realm. They are all willing to help and get this settled once and for all.

We sit down to discuss what our next move should be. We have closed the passageways for the day, ordered a pizza and all settled in for the discussion.

Chase starts. "I think we need to gather everybody that wants to help and surprise attack."

I sigh. "I don't think we are going to have that option. I heard Drake talking to one of the other guards when I opened the passageways this morning. I don't think he realized I had opened it yet. It sounds like they are really close to coming here and attacking. I think we might only have a couple of days."

Landon had been sitting back in his chair listening. "I think we need to get everyone here and then we are prepared. I think you are both right. If we can get everyone here, we will probably be ready about the same time they plan on attacking."

Penelope looks really concerned. "How are we going to explain all these people showing up here? This is a really small town that really doesn't get a lot of visitors. It will really draw attention when all these people start showing up here and are looking for somewhere to stay."

I furrow my brow while I try to figure out a solution. "I have to admit that is going to be really hard to explain. It will also draw a lot of attention that they all know us."

Ethan smiles. "All we have to do is say we invited all of our families here to get to know each other after the weddings. If they are all connected to us somehow, then it would explain why so many of them have all shown up at once and why they all know us."

I grin. "That is a great idea. I will send out emails and making calls. I'm sure we can get everyone here in the next couple of days."

For the next few hours we contact the faeries and trolls that have offered us assistance. Chase and I also go to talk to the dwarves and gnomes to see if they would be willing to help us again.

When we have it all set up, we sit down to discuss it again. I start off the discussion this time.

"Ok, I have gotten the dwarves and gnomes set up and they are ready. I told them it will be tomorrow and I will open the portal for them all to come through."

Landon nods his head. "We have everyone else already here and getting settled. There are a couple more that will be coming in tonight but pretty much everyone else is here and ready. The cover story is going well. Once I told a couple of people about it nobody really questioned it."

Rayne looks bored. "Well since nobody else has brought it up, I guess I will have to. They are all going to feel the power of the Origin when they get there. We are not going to be able to keep the location of the Origin a secret after this. We have invited all the magickal beings in existence to come and experience the power of the Origin."

I sigh at her sarcasm. "I have explained to them all that it is a place of power and not the Origin. I also told them to not be surprised by the amount of power that is there since it is also where the passageways are. I told them that with the combined power of the place of power and the passageways that they would feel a lot of power in the land. They all seemed to think that was a reasonable explanation. Nobody will think it is the Origin because we are having them all come there."

Landon smiles. "Why would we invite them to the one place we want to keep hidden? It is the perfect hiding place. If you hide something in plain sight, then nobody even considers what they are looking for is actually right in front of them."

Rayne rolls her eyes at Landon's explanation. I decide it is best to ignore her sarcasm since it is her way of dealing with the stress of the situation.

"Ok, so everyone is supposed to meet in the clearing in the morning. I have set up portals where the others are staying in town so nobody sees all those people all going out there. It would raise a lot of questions for the normal people in this town to see all these visitors all going out to a secluded area of the woods and hiking in."

We talk for a little bit longer about the plan to make sure we didn't need anything else done. When we are done, I lead Chase to the portal to take us to our beach.

When we walk through the portal, he instantly wraps his arms around my waist and pulls me in close for a kiss. We then turn and watch the beautiful sunset. We watch the stars start to appear in silence for a while.

I raise my eyebrows in question when Chase suddenly turns on his side and lies there and looks at me. "Why are you staring at me?"

He laughs. "I love to watch the look of wonder in your eyes as you watch the stars slowly appear. You know which ones will come out first and you always know where to look to see them as they appear in the night sky, but yet you still watch as if you aren't sure they will actually appear."

I smile. "Just because they have been the ones we have seen so far doesn't mean they always will be. The stars are always changing. Nothing stays the same. If you pay close enough attention, you will notice that each night there is always something a little bit different from the last time. It is slow and you have to watch to notice it, but it's there."

He sighs. "I want you to be careful tomorrow. I know you can take care of yourself but you also like to believe the person you are coming against will see they are wrong and will stop. The faeries and trolls are not going to be like that. They are all going to be coming at you full force. You will be the main target. They think if they can take you out then it will make the rest easy."

I turn on my side so I can face him. "I know they are all coming for me. It makes it easier for the rest of you to get the jump on them. If they are all focused on me, then they won't be watching all of you as closely. They think I am the one with all the power and I need to be taken out, but they don't realize that all of you have as much power as you do. They are going to really underestimate all of you. We have always given them the impression that I am the only one that has the power. We did that on purpose so when it came time they would not really focus on you at all."

He smiles. "I knew there was another reason our parents only wanted you to go to the other realms and why I was told to only protect you but to let you handle things when we went looking for the hybrids. Since all they have seen is us putting you up front and doing all the work, then they will think that is because we can't."

I smile and nod my head. "I'm sorry I couldn't tell you before. Our parents were afraid if you knew then it would look forced when you let me take the lead."

"I can see where that would be a problem." We both roll back to our backs and watch the stars for a little while longer before we head back to the house to get some sleep for the long day we have the next day.

The next morning, we eat breakfast in silence. We are all

caught up in our own thoughts about the day ahead of us and not really in the mood for talking. The animals are all roaming around our feet like they are agitated.

I finally pick Callie up and start to pet her. I look down at her with my brow furrowed. "What's wrong with you this morning? You never act like this." She meows at me and wiggles her way out of my arms. As soon as she lands on the floor her and the other animals all take the portal to the clearing.

I sigh. "I guess that answers my question. Apparently, we are going to need their help today."

We step through the portal with our nerves a little more frayed by the way the animals are acting.

As soon as I open the portals so the others can come to the clearing I gasp and bend over.

Chase is instantly at my side. "Baby, what's wrong?"

I open my arms as Callie jumps to land in them. I then concentrate and everyone watches as I work hard at what I am doing.

I can finally grind out between clenched teeth "The faeries and trolls are both trying to come through the passageways in very high numbers all at the same time. I am trying to shove them back into their realms so I can close the passageways. It is really hard with them both coming at the same time and with how many are in between the realms right now."

Rayne smirks. "Don't worry about the ones that are between the realms. Just close the passageways and trap the ones stuck in between."

I scowl at her. "That won't do any good. As soon as we try to enter their realms, then the ones stuck in between will be there to defend their realm."

As I am still struggling to get them back to their realms everybody else starts to show up. Penelope explains to the others what is going on.

Suddenly I feel a hand on my shoulder. When I look up, I see the faerie man we had met with after his son thought he had captured us. I look to my other side and see one of the troll adults that had been in his group.

I then feel them work with me to send their kind back. The faerie helps me push the other faeries back, and the troll helps me send the other trolls back. It doesn't take long with their help and I am able to get them back to where they belong and slam the passageways closed. The sound of the passageways being slammed closed echoes through the woods.

I turn to thank the faerie and troll for their help but he speaks before I have a chance to.

"They were counting on you not being able to send them all the way back. You can only force that many back at once if you have the help from one from that realm. When you were sending back the ones from the village, you had the Guardians on that side not working against you. This time you had the Guardians pushing them forward, so it was keeping you from being able to fully send them back."

"Thank you for your help. I wasn't sure how much longer I could keep them out of this realm."

He nods his head and walks back over to his group.

I look around at the people gathered to help us and am overwhelmed with emotion by all the people that came to help. The clearing is full of people and they are spilling out into the surrounding trees.

"I want to thank you all for coming to our aide. We know this realm is as much your home as it is ours and we thank you for helping us in defending it."

They all cheer and I continue when they quiet down.

"I have talked to the Guardians in the elf and goblin realms. They have worked with me to seal the passageways from their realms. Nobody is able to enter their realms and the passageway to the fearie realm is only open for us to travel there. We are taking the fight to the faeries. Once the trolls realize that is the only realm that is not closed to them they will know that is where we are going."

When I am sure they all understand, I turn and open the

passageway to the faerie realm to allow us to enter there but not for anyone to enter our realm. We then start pouring through the passageway.

CHAPTER 27

When we come out on the other side we walk into a wall of faeries. It is pretty much what I had expected after them trying to come through the portal. There is a group around Drake and he is desperately trying to reopen the passageway to our realm. The other faeries are not happy with him at all after being shoved back to their realm.

I turn and smile at Chase and then he starts to laugh as the startled faeries go flying. I had sent a wave of magick forth to take some of them out before they overcame their shock.

The last thing the faeries had been expecting was for us to come through the passageway ready to fight them especially with so much help. If the situation had been different, I would have had to laugh at the looks on their faces. They had been expecting to come through and take us completely by surprise and to easily overcome us.

They are all scrambling around and trying to get the advantage when the trolls come through from their realm. The faeries get their confidence back and think they have us trapped between them and the trolls.

I smile as they realize the elves and the goblins had been

waiting for the trolls to come through and they are now pouring in from their realms behind the trolls.

It is the most eerily quiet battle I have ever seen. Everyone is concentrating on their magick and what they are trying to do so there is pretty much no talking at all. We can hear grunts of pain every once in a while, but more often than that we would see someone just fall over. Some were dead and some just badly wounded.

I can't bring myself to actually kill someone. I am draining the magick from the foes I am facing. When their magick has been drained, I will then place them under a deep sleeping spell and they would no longer be a threat to us. I make sure I am using a spell I can reverse and give the magick back to the person if we find they have been forced to fight against us. It is a strong spell and I am the only one who can reverse it. Nobody else will be able to give the magick back to anyone that I have drained.

Chase makes sure he can always see me. He leaves me to fight on my own but he wants to make sure he is right there if I need him.

Callie has been at my feet since I had let her down after we got the faeries and trolls back to their realms. I notice the other animals are staying close to the others as well. It appears our magick is enhanced just by having them next to us. They don't have to be touching us anymore for their helpful boost.

A couple of the faeries and trolls realize the animals are giving us power and they start to go after the animals instead of the person. Just as a troll is sneaking up on Ghost and Chase is distracted with the faerie he is fighting I start to call out. Callie jumps up on the troll's back and digs her claws in. Unfortunately, the troll had already started to throw his magick at Ghost and Callie isn't able to stop him.

I yell as Ghost falls to the ground. Chase instantly feels the loss of the connection with the dog. He turns and sees Ghost lying on the ground. He narrows his eyes at the troll that is still trying to get Callie off his back. Chase puts the anger and hurt at seeing Ghost like that in the magick he throws at the troll. The troll falls to the ground dead. Chase's eyes widen as he realizes what he has done. He has been restraining the faeries and trolls he has fought against and this is the first one he has actually killed.

As the troll hits the ground Callie jumps from his back and runs over to Ghost. We don't have time to check on the dog or to see what Callie is doing. I look over at Chase and see the hurt and anger in his eyes at seeing Ghost like that.

I yell over to him so he can hear me. "Remember what my dad said. As long as we are ok they will be too. Callie will take care of him and he will be fine."

He nods his head and puts the anger and hurt into his next battle. He is dropping faeries and trolls very quickly now. I don't have time to really worry about whether he is killing them or just restraining them.

I have so many of them coming after me I lose track of everybody else. For every one I neutralize two more step up. The Origin is still feeding me power so I am not getting worn out but I know when this is over I am going to really feel the weight of using all this magick.

We are making progress and a lot of faeries and trolls are on the ground when I hear Chase yell to get my attention. When I finally find him in the crowd, he is pointing at something behind me. I turn and see King Blaize and King Sebastian are both standing there watching the battle with smirks on their faces.

I instantly feel the rage take over. I make my way toward them. I can take down any faerie or troll that tries to stop me from getting to the two kings.

When I am close and there is only one line of defense left between me and the kings, the Troll King starts to look scared. The Faerie King still has an amused smirk on his face.

King Sebastian turns to King Blaize. "You must give me some of the power from the Origin. She will be able to overcome us if you don't."

King Blaize laughs. "You will never be able to use the

power from the Origin. It was placed in my realm for me to use. If you were meant to use it, then it would have been placed in your realm."

King Sebastian is instantly furious. "You said we would be equal partners and would rule the realms together. That is not possible if you intend to use the power of the Origin over my head."

I have reached them by this point. "I hope I'm not interrupting an important conversation. King Sebastian I know you are just now figuring out that you were played for a fool but I am ready to finish this so if you don't mind I have some things that I need to discuss with King Blaize."

The Troll King throws magick at me. I sigh and stand there as his magick is absorbed by my shield. When he realizes he is not affecting me whatsoever he smirks as he throws his magick at a goblin that is nearby who is so focused on her faerie opponent that she doesn't even see it coming.

I deflect the spell and send it right back at him. He falls to the ground. It looks like he is unconscious and not dead so I turn my attention to King Blaize.

He looks down at the Troll King and starts to laugh. "Thank you for shutting him up. I was really tired of listening to his whining. Well, I guess my secret is out. Now that you know I have control of the Origin I guess we can talk about your surrender and what your role will be now that I will be ruling over all the realms."

It is my turn to laugh. "If you had ever bothered to verify that what you had was actually the Origin you would have known that all you have is a place of power. You have an area in your realm where magick has collected because there is no one in that area to use it. It isn't even a strong place of power. We have at least ten in our realm that are stronger than yours. We also have the true Origin."

His face turns red as his anger increases with each word I say. "LIAR! You can't possibly have the Origin in your realm. You are the weakest and the least skilled in the use of magick. You wouldn't even know how to use that much power. If you had the Origin, you would have already taken over all the realms."

I sigh. "If you weren't so full of yourself, you would see we have control of the Origin because we wouldn't use it to dominate the other realms or even to dominate our own kind. If you don't want to believe me, that's fine. Draw on your power and take your best shot. I won't do anything other than stand here. If you have the Origin, then you will be able to easily break through my protection spell and then you would have what you want. When you are done, then it will be my turn to take a shot at you."

He smirks and I can feel him drawing from his place of power. The Origin increases the power of my protection shield to stay just over the power that he is drawing. As he continues to draw, it continues to feed.

He finally gets a self-satisfied smirk on his face and prepares to throw his magick at me. The rest of the people that have been battling have all seen what is happening, and they had all stopped to see what the outcome will be between me and the Faerie King.

He throws his magick and I feel it absorb into my protection shield. It really is a lot of power but we still have many more powerful places of power in our realm.

His eyes widen in shock as I stand there and grin at him. "My turn." I don't even draw any more power than what the Origin has already put into my magick to protect me from the King.

His face loses all color as he feels his magick being bound inside of him. I have decided not to take his magick away. I am binding it in him so he can still feel it but he cannot access it or use it in any way.

The others that have been watching don't make a sound. They can't tell what is going on. All they can see is the Troll King on the ground unconscious, the Faerie King obviously fighting a battle he isn't winning and me standing there with a smile on my face.

Chase walks up to me. "Baby, I think you have proven

your point."

I turn to him. "I'm not doing anything anymore. I bound his power inside of him so he can feel it but not use it. The rest he is doing to himself. The more he tries to use his power the weaker he gets. If he would accept what has happened and agree to be reasonable, then we could move on."

Chase laughs. "Only you would think to do something like that. What makes you think he will ever be reasonable?"

I look around at everyone watching and waiting to see what will happen. "The Troll King is only unconscious but when he wakes, he will not be able to use his magick any more than the Faerie King will at this time. Until we come to an agreement with all the realms for a peaceful existence that does not leave any realm watching over their shoulders there will be no magick used by any faeries or trolls."

I sigh as I see some of the other races use this to their advantage against some of the faeries and trolls that are standing there in shock as they realize they really can't use their magick.

"All right let me amend that. Until we come to an agreement, none of you will be able to use magick. You couldn't leave well enough alone so you brought this on yourselves. The only ones that still have the ability to use magick is the Guardians of the Passageways. That includes anyone from my realm."

The gnomes that have been smirking suddenly are very pouty. I think they had been planning to use this magickal ban to their advantage.

I turn to the Faerie King who is still trying to use his magick against me. I roll my eyes at him. "You might as well give up before you wear yourself out. I would like to sit down with all the leaders and come to an agreement as soon as possible so the magickal ban can come to an end."

Just then our parents appear. My dad speaks for them. "I agree. This needs to be settled immediately so everyone can get back to their lives."

The Faerie King is glaring at my dad. "You can't come to

my realm and take our magick and demand we work with you."

My dad sighs. "You were planning on doing that to everyone else and besides we just did."

The Faerie King stares at him with his mouth hanging open.

CHAPTER 28

Since we are already in the faerie realm we decide this is as good a place as any to have the meeting. The queens from the elf and goblin realms come through the passageways.

The Elf Queen smiles as she approaches us. My mom grins. "Queen Thalia, it is so nice to see you again. I wish it was under better circumstances."

Queen Thalia laughs. "I think these are the best circumstances. It is way past time to get this whole thing settled. I don't like all the negativity from all the distrust of the faeries and the trolls. If we can get a clear understanding of how things will work from now on it will be so much better."

"I agree with you. It is time to come to an agreement."

The Goblin Queen walks up and I smile. "Queen Genevieve is the spell we did still working for you?"

She beams. "Oh, yes. It's wonderful. Thank you so much. I could never repay you for the kindness you have shown us."

King Blaize scrunches up his nose. "I don't welcome the goblins or their smell in my castle."

I narrow my eyes at him. "If you would get off your high

horse, you would realize they no longer have that smell. We took the time to investigate and find the problem and help them to correct it. Unlike you who shunned them instead of trying to help them. It's no wonder your faeries are the most hated of all the magickal beings."

He is working up into a good rant but my dad speaks before he has a chance to. "Annisa, that kind of attitude will not help."

The King has a satisfied grin on his face until my dad turns to him. "King Blaize if you continue to have that kind of attitude we may have to close all the passageways to and from your realm so you and your faeries will not be permitted to any of the other realms."

He loses his smile and I try to hide mine behind my hand as I pretend to cough.

Dad sighs. "All right, let's all go to the castle and sit down and figure out what we can do to get this situation resolved."

We head to the castle. All the others have all gone back to their own realms until we come to an agreement. The passageways have been temporarily closed. All the Guardians from all the realms are attending this meeting. While most of them will not really take part in the meetings, they are there for the protection of their ruler.

When we get in the room the King has indicated would be used for this purpose, he scowls as my dad takes the spot at the head of the room showing he is the one that will run this meeting.

King Blaize doesn't like that at all. "This is my castle and I am the one in charge of what happens in my realm."

My dad smiles. "If that is how you feel then we will all go to another realm and work out an agreement and leave you and your faeries to your own devices here in your realm where you rule."

The King narrows his eyes at my dad. "Threatening me that you will prevent us from traveling every time you don't get what you want will not work."

Dad sighs. "I am not trying to dictate to you what will

happen by threatening you. I am simply trying to show you that if you are not willing to work with us, that is what is going to happen. I have no intention of saying how things will go. I plan on us all putting in our opinions and working out an agreement that works for everyone involved."

He can't argue with that without looking like he is being uncooperative, so he drops in the chair to my dad's right with a scowl on his face and arms crossed over his chest. I stifle my laughter, lean over and whisper in Chase's ear, "If he can't be the leader then he will be the right-hand man."

Chase hides his laugh under a cough. My dad looks at us. He knows since we self heal we never get sick so the coughing is covering up for something. I smile innocently at him and he decides it is not worth asking right now.

He then looks out at the group that has gathered. "You have all been working for as long as you can remember to prevent the faeries from taking over your realms. This is something we want to prevent. We don't want the other realms to feel they have to limit the faeries or they can't trust any faerie. From what I can tell there are no faeries that have found love outside of their own realm. I think that is because they have all been viewed as being the enemy. You didn't feel that it was a good idea to give them any foothold at all in your realms and your people did not feel welcome in their realm."

King Blaize looks around challenging everyone in the room. "My faeries simply are better than the other races and they don't feel it is possible find a suitable mate outside our realm."

The other rulers start to snicker and my dad gets a knowing smirk on his face.

King Blaize looks around confused. "What is so funny?"

Queen Thalia fills him in. "Many of your faeries do not feel that way. Many of them sneak over to our realms to see the loves that you do not allow them. Many of them have secret families in our realms they have never been allowed to acknowledge in your realm. They never asked for permission to stay because they knew you would deny them and then punish them for even asking."

King Blaize looks around shocked. "That can't be true. That is just what they are telling the naïve in your realm. It is just a story they are using to get what they want out of the other person." He sounds like he is trying to convince himself of that more than us.

King Sebastian is sitting in his chair trying not to draw attention to himself. It seems he can't resist the opportunity to make the Faerie King more uncomfortable though. "It is very much true. There are quite a few in my realm as well. I don't see it as a problem." He smirks showing how much he enjoyed delivering this blow to the Faerie King.

My dad sighs and tries to get the conversation back on track. "Now that we know for certain the faeries will not have a problem intermingling with the other realms it will make things easier. It also shows that closing the faerie realm to the other realms is not a solution. We don't want to separate those faeries from their families in the other realms."

King Blaize lets out a defeated sigh. "I want to work something out so that my faeries can be happy. I didn't realize that any of this was happening."

We all look at him with mistrust on our faces. King Sebastian isn't buying it. "You cannot manipulate this situation to better your situation. They have the Origin and you will never have the power it would take to win and take over all the realms. When you agree this time, it will be knowing you will have to follow this agreement. I am ready to put all of this behind us and move on. I am tired of the constant planning and trying to get the upper hand. We need to come to an agreement and all of us live without trying to overtake each other."

King Blaize has been working on a new plan until he hears he lost the support of the trolls. Now when he lets out his breath he seems to shrink in his chair. "What kind of agreement?"

Queen Thalia is so excited she is bouncing in her chair.

"Finally, this is the day that I have always hoped would come. I feel so bad for the elves in my realm that have to wait until their love can visit from the faerie realm again. It will be so much better when these families can finally be together."

King Blaize looks at her shocked. "You mean that was true? I thought you had said that to prove a point. I didn't realize there really were families that were kept apart. I would never want one of my faeries to not be with their children."

She looks at him sadly. "Yes, there are children with faerie and elf parents that are not being raised by both parents. It is not by the choice of the parents but by your beliefs. The faeries come as often as they can and the elf parents have been able to lead the children to believe that the other parent has to travel for work so the children do not feel like there is something wrong with them. Nobody wants their child to think they are not good enough for anything. The children that have grown to adulthood have found they are not welcome with the faeries and have come to resent them for that but the young ones are not told everything so they don't feel like they are being shunned."

King Blaize actually looks ashamed of his behavior. "I had no idea. I knew that some faeries were having relationships in other realms but I didn't realize any children had resulted from those relationships. As a father myself I couldn't imagine not being able to be with my children. We will fix this problem immediately. As soon as this meeting is over, I will send notice to all the faeries telling them if they have children in another realm they are to immediately marry the other parent and they can either choose one realm or both to live in."

We all look at him in shock. Queen Genevieve asks, "You would let a goblin and the children they have with a faerie live in your realm without ridicule or undue hardships?"

He nods his head and adamantly states, "I will not keep my faeries from their children. If they are happy with a goblin and they have children with a goblin or any others from any of the realms, then they need to do what is right. I have been obsessed with beliefs that have been passed down to me. Now that I have realized what I have been taught to believe is not reality I plan to correct my mistakes. I truly didn't know there were children involved. I would never wish that kind of hardship on a child."

My dad says, "Well, that is a very good start. If we can keep this kind of progress going it won't take us long to come up with an agreement. I do want to add though King Blaize just because you have made this declaration does not mean that all of your faeries will feel the same way. There are many who will be relieved by this as this will allow them to be with their families there are still going to be some that were taught the same beliefs as you were. There will still be some that will not welcome the other realms and the children from the unions of faeries and beings from the other realms. How do you plan to prevent this? We can't allow children to come here if they are going to be put in a dangerous situation."

King Blaize holds his head high. "If any of my faeries are unfair or cruel to any child or being choosing to live in this realm, they will be punished in the same manner as if they had committed the acts against another faerie. I do not allow that kind of behavior between my faeries and I will not allow it with any child or adult from another realm. Being punished for loving a faerie or having a faerie parent is not something I will tolerate."

It takes us all a minute to overcome our shock at the King's declaration.

CHAPTER 29

I have to bite the inside of my cheek to keep from laughing as I look over at Rayne and see her struggling to refrain from giving her sarcastic commentary during the meeting. I notice the look her mom is giving her and realize that is the reason that she is working so hard to refrain from saying anything. Her mom is watching her with a scowl on her face clearly indicating she wants Rayne to keep her comments to herself.

My dad glances over a few times and seems amused that she is having such a hard time not making her comments.

King Sebastian is still a little bitter about how things happened at the battle that took place. "I think we need to come up with something that does not include any of us rulers being incapacitated. It is not safe for our realms to have our rulers made so vulnerable."

Rayne can't hold it in any longer. "You are just upset that a puny little witch girl could walk up and render you unconscious in a matter of seconds."

Dad rolls his eyes and tries not to laugh and Renae shoots daggers at Rayne with her eyes. Rayne shrugs her shoulders not apologizing or looking the least bit sorry. "Somebody had to say it."

This time it is my entire group that has to pretend to cough to cover up our laughing. Rayne grins at us knowing exactly what we are doing.

Dad decides it is best to ignore us and move on. "I can understand your concern but today that is exactly what was needed to stop all the useless fighting. The situation had gotten way out of hand and needed to be stopped. That was the quickest and most effective way to end it all."

The Troll King nods his head. "I understand why that approach was taken this time but I would ask that in the future there is another alternative. I don't believe we will have a situation such as this again and simply don't want your Guardians to feel they can bind our magick anytime we do something they do not agree with."

"I agree that would be an unfair an unjustified use of magick. I can agree that will not be something that is used on a wide scale basis as it was today. I however, will not forbid them from using that on a single being if the need arises. If they are being attacked or find someone abusing their magick to harm another, they will bind their magick and bring them forward to face their punishment after we have looked into the situation. If it is unclear whether or not the person they see using their magick to harm another is justified in doing so or not. They will bind the magick of all involved until the matter can be investigated."

"I can agree to that. I would like to clarify they are not allowed to bind the magick of any king or queen. If they feel we are not following our agreement they are to notify you so you can investigate and then we can meet to determine what needs to be done. I feel it should be a meeting like this to make that determination."

"That sounds fair. If any of you feel you are not being treated fairly or if you feel that another ruler is not following the agreement any of you can call another meeting to discuss the situation and a determination can be made from there."

Everyone agrees to this proposal. Now it is getting to the

details part of the meeting that I think will not go well.

My dad must feel the same way because he takes a deep breath and continues, "We all have agreements and contracts for travel between the realms. I think that those now need adjusted. We have all limited the faeries and the trolls knowing that they had ulterior motives. Now that this has all been settled I think we need to come up with one simple contract that will apply to everyone."

I look around and see hesitation on the part of the Elf Queen as well as the Goblin Queen.

Queen Genevieve is the first to voice her concerns. "I understand we are trying to move on and put all of this behind us but I need to make sure that my goblins are protected. Now that we no longer have the stench in our realm I need assurance that the faeries will not come there and attempt to bully or overcome my goblins. It has been generations that we have had this problem and I have a hard time believing King Blaize has had such a sudden change of heart."

We all look to the King Blaize expecting him to be angry and lash out at the tiny Goblin Queen.

It comes as a big surprise to all of us when he looks embarrassed. "I understand why you feel that way and I deserve your mistrust. I have done nothing except prove to you that I can't be trusted. All I can do is give you my word and agree to the terms of another meeting such as this if you feel that I am not fulfilling my end of the agreement."

Everyone in the room stares at him with open mouths for a minute. Then my dad looks over at the Goblin Queen to see her response.

She continues to look at the Faerie King for another couple of minutes and Queen Thalia seems to be studying him.

Queen Genevieve then looks to Queen Thalia and asks, "What do you think?"

"I believe he is telling the truth. I think he is sincere in his assertions. I don't get the feeling that he is doing anything to deceive us. I have been reading his aura since we arrived and the only time I saw deception or cunning was before he found out about the children. Since he learned about the half faerie children that were being raised with no knowledge of their faerie heritage I have seen only regret and good intentions."

I narrow my eyes at her. She grins with mischief in her eyes. "I can read an aura and determine the intentions of another. I always know when I am being lied to or if someone is only telling me a portion of the truth. I also know if someone is telling me what they believe to be true but are using it in a way to manipulate me."

"Wow that would be useful."

She laughs. "Yes, it does come in handy in times like this. Queen Genevieve and I have been friends for a very long time. I once tried to help with the smell in her realm as well. I thought with how connected we are to the earth that I might be able to determine the source but I was never able to figure it out. We value each other's opinion and will often times discuss issues and come to an agreement that benefits us both."

My dad smiles. "I am hoping to someday create that kind of cooperation between all the realms and not just the two of you. This is the kind of relationship we should all have. We need to be helping each other not trying to find ways to bring the others down."

King Sebastian has been sitting there taking this all in. "I agree that an alliance between all of us would be much more useful than the current animosity. I for one would like to learn from the elves how they can be so connected with the earth and use her power so readily. We are powerful but we use the power like a tool I admire the way that you make it part of you and use it in harmony."

Queen Thalia smiles proudly. "You have to thank the earth for lending you the power that you require. You can't take without giving something back. It is all about being grateful and thanking the earth for sharing her gift. The reason it feels like a tool to you is because that is how you see it. We see it as a gift from the earth and use it as such."

He nods his head thoughtfully.

I raise my eyebrows in surprise to see he is taking what she said so seriously. It looks like he is really thinking about what she said and how to do it.

The Elf Queen notices it as well. "I would be happy to meet with you at any time and teach you our methods. I'm sure there are things I could learn from you and your methods as well."

He smiles. "I would appreciate that. We will talk after the meeting and set something up for us to meet and see what we can learn from each other."

My dad smiles happy that the other rulers are working together. "That is a really good idea. I think it would be a good idea for every one of the leaders to meet on a one-on-one basis and see what they can learn. Unfortunately, we will not be able to participate as we are still trying to repair the damage created by the previous Counsel but Annisa could take our place. As we trained her and she is the most powerful of our kind, you can learn as much from her as she can from you. She will then be able to bring what she learns back to the others in our realm."

By the look on his face I can tell that Chase is about to lose his temper. Before he has a chance to say anything my dad continues, "Of course anytime you meet with Annisa her husband Chase will be there as well. It is not personal he just doesn't like it when she is dealing with magickal issues by herself. He even wants to be there when she works with us."

The other leaders laugh. Queen Thalia looks over at Chase. "You will soon learn that she can take care of herself. I understand you wanting to be protective of her but you want to be careful not to hold on so tight that you suffocate her."

I give him a smirk. He looks back over at the Elf Queen. "I appreciate your advice. I must admit she has been telling me the same thing. I am working on not being so protective and have improved some. I admit I still have a way to go."

Rayne can't resist getting her comment in this time since it is at Chase's expense and won't cause problems with the other realms. "Yeah, you have gone from completely cutting her off from everything around her to just letting her out of your sight for more than an hour at a time. Big improvement."

Chase scowls at her while everyone else in the room bursts out in laughter.

When the laughter has calmed down Chase mumbles, "There is nothing wrong with wanting to keep you safe."

King Sebastian looks at him with sympathy. "You are right there is nothing wrong with wanting to keep her safe. There is a thin line between keeping her safe and obsessing and not letting her experience life. If you obsess and cut her off from everything she will end up resenting you and will be at more of a risk as she fights against you to gain her freedom."

I give Chase a knowing look while he looks at the Troll King with surprise. He nods his head to acknowledge the advice, and the meeting moves on to the next subject.

We spend the next couple of hours going through the details that each ruler wants. We are able to come up with an agreement that everybody is happy with. Each party has to give up a few things. With everyone compromising we come up with something that benefits everyone.

CHAPTER 30

When we get home, Chase starts to pace. We sit on the couch and watch him. We are patiently waiting for him to be ready to talk about what it is that has him so agitated. I have no idea what it could be since the meeting went so well.

He keeps pacing mumbling things like, "I don't like it. There must be something they are not saying. I know there is something they are after."

After about an hour my amusement at him is starting to wane. I am tired of him focusing on whatever crazy idea he has going through his head now.

Apparently, my dad feels the same way. "Chase, enough. Either sit down and talk to us or get over it. You have been pacing and mumbling to yourself for an hour now."

Chase spins and glares at my dad. "I can't believe you are so calm about this. They are trying to get to her and you are sitting there and letting them. They are working out a plan to take her and you are playing right into their hands."

I jump up completely pissed and ready to tell him what I think about his assumption that I am some helpless girl that is being taken advantage of.

I don't get the chance to say anything because my dad

beats me to it. He stands and glares right back at Chase. "Just because you are so insecure and think that you are the only one that can protect Annisa does not give you the right to talk to me like that. She is my daughter and I would never agree to something that would put her in danger."

"You already have. You took her parading through all the realms and showing them exactly what she looks like and who they need to go after. You served her up on a silver platter saying here is the one you need to take to get control of our realm."

"I took her to the realms to show them she is not some helpless little girl being kept in a tower that they can come and take whenever they wanted. I took her there to show them she is not going to sit here and let them walk all over her."

"You set her up to be taken away from me."

I have had enough. "I AM RIGHT HERE! Both of you sit down." I cross my arms over my chest and waited for them to do as I say. They had both spin when I yell at them. When they get over the shock of me interrupting in such a loud way, they both sit down and look at me.

"I am not a trophy or a possession. I am also not some damsel in distress that needs saving. I am a powerful witch that has the ability to take care of myself. I don't need you parading me around for whatever statement you want to make any more than I need you to protect me from the big bad faeries. You both need to realize that you will not control me and you will not dictate to me what I will do."

My dad knows better than to say anything when I am this mad. Chase thinks he needs to make me see things his way. "You don't see what they are doing. You always want to believe the best in people so you are letting them convince you that they really want this to work. They want to work with you and figure out what your weaknesses are so they can take you and gain control of the Origin."

I narrow my eyes at him and am so furious that I can feel my pulse pounding in my head. "I am not some stupid little girl that will believe anything that anyone tells me. Yes, I want to believe the best in people but that doesn't make me some helpless little girl that will let anyone lead me around with whatever they want to tell me. I can tell when I am being lied to. If you think I am so weak that I will be taken and only you can protect me from that then you don't really know me at all."

With that I spin on my heel and storm out of the room. Chase tries to follow me and explain but I use magick to hold him in his seat and keep his mouth closed so he can't talk.

I hear Rayne and Penelope following me out. Rayne laughs as she says, "Chase, you will never learn. You can't treat her like a little kid she has more power than you."

I can hear him mumbling trying to talk even though his mouth won't open. Just as I get to the door it slams closed. I spin around and fix my furious glare on him.

Rayne can't help herself after being so quiet in the meeting. "Really, you need to think before you act. I can't wait to see what she does to you next, moron."

As I am glaring at him, the door shatters and the pieces rearrange themselves around him to enclose him in a wooden bubble. So now not only can he not get up from the chair, can't talk but he also can't see through the wood that has encapsulated him.

I spin on my heel and leave the room with a laughing Rayne and Penelope behind me. I hear Landon laughing and say, "Dude, you are really going to have to learn that she will not let you decide for her. She is stubborn and will not tolerate it even from you. I doubt she will let you out for a while so you better get used to sitting there."

I am still so furious that I think it would be better to be outside instead of in the house where I can really do some damage. I walk out and past the pool. I stop in the big open area of the yard where we practice our magick.

Rayne is still laughing. "You will really have to teach me how to do that. That was great!"

I look at her, not sure what my reaction is going to be.

"You think it's great that my husband thinks I am some helpless little girl that needs her big strong husband to protect her so she doesn't get hurt by the big bad faeries?"

"No, Miss Pissy, I think it's great that you put him in his place and didn't let him treat you like that. You actually made me proud. There was no trying to explain to him what he was doing is wrong and trying to reason with him. You had a genuine bitch fit, and it was epic!"

Penelope laughs. "It was pretty great. He looked so surprised when you blew up. He actually thought he was going to explain and you would be fine with it. I don't think he knew what you were getting so mad about."

I scowl. "He will have plenty of time to think about it while he is stuck on that chair surrounded by the door he tried to use against me. I can't believe he thought he could slam the door and I would be fine with it at all. Did he actually think I would stay in there because he slammed the door? Really, like I couldn't get through a closed door!"

Rayne is still giggling. "How long are you going to leave him there?"

I am still seething. "I don't know yet. He was being such an ass. My dad will be surprised when he realizes he can't leave the room either. If he thought he was going to get out of dealing with me after announcing that he paraded me around to show the other realms that he would not tolerate them messing with me then he will soon figure out that won't happen."

Penelope smirks. "Well, since you won't let him open the connection with you he is now pleading with me to make you come back in the house. He said it's not safe for you to be out here and that you need to come back in."

"I can't believe that he would say something like that right now. Does he really think I am that helpless?"

Rayne is no longer amused. "Oh, and of course you wouldn't have any help if someone came after you because Penelope and I are just girls like you so what could we possibly do to help?"

I can hear my dad yelling from the house. He must have figured out that he can't leave the living room.

My mom comes out of the house laughing. "Well you certainly know how to make a point. Do you feel better?"

I scowl. "No, Chase is telling Penelope through the connection that we need to go back inside because it isn't safe for me to be out here. I swear he has mashed potatoes for brains."

She laughs. "Your father is not handling being trapped in that room any better. I think it's good for both of them. Why don't you leave them in there and us girls will go out for dinner and do a little shopping."

I smile and we get our purses and the other moms and head for the door. All the guys except for Chase and my dad are doing other things in the house and said for us to have fun. The only request they make is that I put a soundproof spell on the room so they didn't have to listen to my dad yell the whole time we are gone. I gladly put the spell on.

I open the connection enough for me to speak to Chase but he can't say anything back. *"I am going out with the girls you can sit there and try and figure out why you are there. I hope by the time I get back you will be ready to treat me like I deserve to be treated."* I then slam the connection closed letting him know I am blocking him out and he will not be able to get in.

Penelope and Rayne start to laugh. Rayne looks over at me. "You had to put salt in the wound, didn't you? Telling him you were going out with the girls so he will know there are no guys with you. He is in a panic. I'm glad I can close the connection and not have to listen to him. Ethan says he closed it a while ago when Chase kept trying to convince him that he needs to be outside with us because we weren't safe out there."

Penelope smiles. "Landon said the same thing. I closed the connection outside so all I could feel was him trying to get in but didn't hear about you telling him you were going out with the girls."

Rachael sighs. "I don't know what has gotten into him. I

certainly didn't raise him to treat you like that. He deserves every ounce of what you are giving him. I can't believe he thinks this is an acceptable way to treat you. I will be talking to him when we get back. I'm sure you won't mind letting me give him a piece of my mind before you get a hold of him."

I smile. "I have absolutely no problem letting you talk to him first. Maybe then he will get his head out of his ass and use his brain."

My mom laughs. "I will let you have at your father first. I think he will know way before we get back what it was he did wrong. I know he only thinks he was protecting you but he went too far this time. You give him hell honey."

We have a great time blowing off steam with a fun dinner and a shopping trip to the mall. We try on funny hats and are really goofy. It is fun to act silly and hang out with my best friends and our moms for a while.

We also do some shopping for clothes. It is great to have so many of us finding things that would look good on each other. We are able to find some things that we never would have found ourselves. Our moms actually have a really good sense of fashion and are great at picking things out for us to try on.

CHAPTER 31

We have a great time so when we get home I'm not nearly as angry as when we left. The guys laugh when we get back hours later.

Landon walks up and gives Penelope a kiss. "Did you have fun?"

She smiles. "It was great. We need to do a girl's day like that more often."

He laughs. "I think it's a great idea but you get to tell Chase about it." He then looks over at me with amusement in his eyes. "You know he is panicking thinking someone took you right? I had to shut the connection because he wouldn't listen when I told him you would be fine and you girls don't need us guys with you to protect you."

I wince. "I'm sorry you had to deal with him. I will take care of it."

He gets serious. "I don't mind. He needs to realize that you can't be put in a bubble and kept away from everyone and everything. He also needs to understand that you can protect yourself. After you girls are done with him I plan on having a long talk with him myself. I won't sit back and watch him treat you like that. He has to know that he can't act like that."

"Thank you, Landon."

He squeezes my arm and him and Penelope walk away. Mom and I walk to the doorway to the room that my dad and Chase are in.

I can't see Chase because the door is still surrounding him. My dad looks up and I can tell by the look in his eyes that he has used the time to think about what had pissed me off. He stands up as we walk into the room.

"Before you say anything I have something to explain to you. I will not be paraded around for you to prove a point. I do not need you to protect me from the world. I understand I am your only child and you are protective. You need to understand that I am a grown woman and very powerful and I can take care of myself. You and mom raised me to be strong and independent. You have to let go and trust me to make my own way."

He nods his head. Then he walks over and envelopes me in a hug. "I'm so sorry, sweetheart. You're right. I wasn't thinking. All I could see was you were my baby girl, and they were all going to be coming for you. I know you can handle it and you are strong enough to take care of yourself. I promise I won't do anything like this again. Just so you know I tried to talk to Chase, and I explained to him why you were so upset but I don't know if he actually listened to anything I said."

"Thanks for trying dad. I will make sure he understands what he did."

He laughs as he looks over my shoulder at my mom. "I'm sure you will sweetheart. Just give him some slack he is trying. Now I have to go listen to the lecture your mom has for me about how you are no longer a little girl that needs her daddy watching over her." He winks at me and follows my mom out of the room.

I sigh and put the door back together and on the hinges. I close it softly and look at Chase for a minute. Then I sit in the chair facing him. He is glaring at me clearly still very angry.

I take a deep breath. "I'm going to leave your mouth closed so I can say what I have to say to you then I will release you. I refuse to be treated like you treated me today. I don't care what you thought you were doing. I don't care that you think you need to protect me. You are going to realize that I don't need you to protect me and I don't have to have you connected to my hip at all times in order to be safe. If you don't realize this, then I don't see how our marriage is going to work."

His eyes widen at my last statement. I shake my head and continue.

"If you insist on treating me like I am helpless and can't do anything to protect myself, then we are going to do nothing but fight. I refuse to live like that. I love you but if you don't respect me, then this will never work."

I release the magick I had been using on him. He instantly starts to talk. "I can't believe you would do that to me. You think you can trap me here, not let me speak, close the connection so I can't even make sure you are all right and then come in here and tell me that my actions will be what tears us apart? What in the world would make you think that me keeping you safe and here with me is treating you with no respect?"

"The fact that you still don't see what you did as wrong is a huge problem. Until you are ready to talk about this rationally I don't have anything else to say to you."

I get up and walk out of the room. He sits there and stares at me with his mouth hanging open. Landon had come back at some point and is waiting outside the door. He puts his hand on my shoulder and gives an encouraging squeeze as he passes and steps into the room to talk to Chase.

Mom must have given dad the short lecture because she is waiting out there as well. She leads me into the next room and wraps me in a comforting hug. The stress of the last few days catches up with me and I start to cry. My mom holds me for quite some time until I am all cried out.

When I am done, she puts her hands on my cheeks. "Honey, I know it's really hard for you right now. I promise it will get better. You and Chase will work through this. You are both still adjusting to all of this. There are going to be some rocky spots. Your father and I still have our tough patches. What matters is that you love each other and you don't give up."

I give her a sad smile. "I know mom but he doesn't even understand what he did wrong. He thinks he was justified in what he did."

"Oh honey, he doesn't really think that. He is scared. He has experienced what it feels like when you were taken away from him. He is willing to do anything to keep that from happening again. He is acting out of fear. He will come around and it will all work out."

"I hope so, because I can't live without him and I can't live with him acting like that. He was doing so much better. I don't understand."

My head snaps around as I hear Chase clear his throat in the doorway. I narrow my eyes at him.

Mom gives me another hug and walks out of the room. She gives Chase's arm a gentle squeeze on her way out.

When she leaves the room Chase walks in and closes the door. He doesn't have the look of pure fury that he had when I had talked to him earlier.

He stands there and stares at me for a minute. Then he takes a deep breath. "I'm sorry I got so crazy. It was the thought of that damn Faerie King coming and trying to take you to get control of the Origin."

"Why would you think that? He never gave any impression that he had planned anything like that."

"I know, I just know how sneaky he can be. It has happened before. Everybody thinks if they have you they have the power. I just got it in my head he was only agreeing to all of this to get us to let our guard down so he could take you."

I groan. "You can't think that everyone we deal with is

going to try and take me. Besides you saw what I did out there. If I can bind the magick of every magickal being all at once then I think I can handle one Faerie King and whoever he sends to take me. I'm not some helpless little girl that needs you to protect me."

He sighs. "I know, but I am the guy and I am the one that is supposed to take care of you."

I raise my eyebrows. "While I what, clean the house and take care of the children? This isn't the 50's Chase. I can do more than raise the kids and care for the house. Besides, we have a service that comes in to clean the house so I would get really bored really fast."

He rolls his eyes. "Of course, that isn't what I expect you to do. I know you will not stay in the house all the time but is it really too much to ask that I be with you whenever you leave the house?"

"Yes, it is. There is no need for me to be held prisoner."

His eyes widen in surprise and he takes a step back. "I'm not holding you prisoner."

I sigh again. "Yes, you are. I can't go anywhere without your permission and only if you can go with me. Other than that, I have to stay in the house where you can keep an eye on me. How is that not like being a prisoner?"

He stammers for a minute while he tries to come up with an answer. "Ok, fine I see your point. I get so crazy thinking that something could happen to you and I won't be there to help."

"If you only wanted to help that would be one thing, but that is not what you are trying to do. You are trying to control my every move and dictate what I can and can't do. I refuse to be in a relationship like that."

"That isn't what I'm trying to do. Landon explained it to me that even though that's not what I was trying to do that was what I was doing. I never wanted to control you I just wanted to keep you safe. I see how those have intertwined."

"Did the fact that you were forced to stay on a chair with your mouth closed while surrounded by the pieces of a door for hours give you any clue that I can take care of myself? I have the power to do that. I also have the ability to create a portal so you can be where I am in a matter of seconds if I need help. I can use the connection to let you know I need help and give you a way to get to me quickly. That will have to be enough."

"I'm trying, baby, give me credit for that. It is so hard for me to watch all of this going on and you having to deal with so much. I think that sometimes you want things to go a certain way and you just believe that they will. You don't even consider that someone could be doing something to work against you or could be plotting against you."

"I know there is always someone plotting against me. If I got worked up over that, then I would never get anything done. I have to go with what is in front of me at the time. Believe me I know things will go wrong and there are times that I am going to really have to fight to get things to go right, but I have to deal with it as it comes. I know that not everyone will have the same motivation as I do and that not everyone deserves for me to think the best of them. Sometimes I have to give them the benefit of the doubt and hope they come through."

"It's the ones that don't come through that worry me. You give them the opportunity to really hurt you and don't seem to even notice."

I laugh. "You need to pay closer attention. I notice and I always have a backup plan to protect us. I may give them the benefit of the doubt but I am always prepared for them to disappoint me."

He looks at me surprised.

I smile. "I told you, you just have to trust me. I'm not as naïve as you like to think I am."

He crosses the room and wraps himself around me. "Please don't ever threaten to leave me again. I can't live without you."

"That wasn't a threat. I meant every word I said to you. I love you but I can't live like that."

He leans back and looks into my eyes. I let the sincerity of that statement flow. He wraps himself around me again. "Baby, give me the chance to make this right."

CHAPTER 32

We open the door to find Rachael leaning against the wall with her arms crossed over her chest. One look at the expression on her face and Chase sighs as he turns and walks back into the room. I sit down to watch as his mom lets him know what she thinks about his behavior.

I can feel the anger rolling off of her. She pins Chase with her glare and doesn't hold back how she feels.

"You were not raised to treat your wife like that. I can't believe you thought that was acceptable behavior."

Chase tries to say something but she won't let him.

"I'm not done. You will stand there and listen until I am finished with what I have to say. You are my son and I love you very much but I will not sit back and watch as you treat Annisa like that. I don't care if you are soul mates. Just because you are soul mates doesn't mean you get to treat her any way you want to, and she has to stay. I was ready to help her move her stuff out of your room after the way you behaved today. How would you feel if Landon treated Penelope like that? You wouldn't like it anymore than the rest of us like it when you do it to Annisa. I thought when you learned your lesson last time when the whole mess with the passageways happened but I guess you didn't."

Chase is finally able to interrupt her rant. "Mom, I'm sorry. I have already apologized to Annisa. I know I can't act like that. I just got so crazy thinking the Faerie King would try and take her away from me. I promise I will do better."

"You're damn right you will do better. I raised you to treat her with respect and to help her not suffocate her. I was appalled by your behavior. You have never seen your dad treat me like that so I don't know where you got the crazy idea that it was all right. You may be grown and married but I am still your mother and I will not tolerate you behaving like that."

He reaches over and gives her a hug. "Ok, mom I get it. It won't happen again."

She scowls at him and starts to leave the room. Chase looks over at me and says, "Well that sucked."

I laugh. "You might want to get comfortable you're not done yet."

He looks at me confused until the door opens again and his sister walks in just as pissed as their mom had been.

Chase braces himself for what he knows is coming.

Penelope narrows her eyes at him with her hands on her hips. "After all the shit, we have dealt with and everything we have overcome, I can't believe you would do something so stupid. You finally have it right and are with the one person you are meant to be with and you try and throw it all away by being a male chauvinistic pig. The way you acted today was so horrible that I was actually ashamed you were my brother."

Chase flinches like she slapped him.

She notices. "I don't care how much that hurt. Do you have any idea what you put her through today? Do you realize she was in here with her mom for over an hour and a half? And that was after we had taken her out to distract her and let her calm down. There is no excuse for the way you acted. If you ever do anything even remotely like that again I will personally make your life hell."

He sighs. "Penelope, I promise I have learned my lesson

this time. I won't do anything to risk losing her. You know how crazy I can get when it comes to her."

"I don't care how crazy you can get when it comes to her. You need to control that. Give her the credit she has earned. She has proven time and again that she can handle whatever is thrown at her."

"I know. I will do better."

"You better."

She leaves the room and Chase lets out a sigh of relief.

I laugh. "I wouldn't be too relieved yet."

He looks at me confused. "Why not?"

From the doorway, my mom says, "Because it's my turn now."

Chase looks at my mom with a look of panic in his eyes. He knows how to handle his mom and sister and knows they will forgive him. He knew exactly what to say to them to calm them down and get them to let it go. My mom is a different story.

She looks at him. "Sit down. I have a few things I want to tell you and I won't be as easy to pacify as your mom and sister were."

He looks at me and I smile at him from my chair. I don't feel sorry for him at all. He has brought all of this on himself. I also know that my mother can be as protective of me as my dad and my husband. She only chooses to intervene when it is something that she feels needs her intervention.

Chase realizes that I will not offer him any help and sits in a chair with a defeated sigh.

Mom sits across from him. "I sat in here with my daughter while she cried herself out for over an hour."

Chase's head snaps around to look at me but mom isn't done yet.

"I know where your behavior was coming from but that does not excuse it. I have raised my daughter to be strong and independent. She loves you and wants to be with you. I can understand the need to protect her. Her father and I also have that need. You need to understand that in order to protect her you have to trust her. She is stubborn but if she needs help, she will ask for it. Your situation is one that comes with a lot of insecurities. You have your memories of your past lives and all that has gone wrong. I understand how you can panic when it comes to her. What you need to understand is that none of that matters."

He looks at her really confused. "I don't understand."

She takes a deep breath. "You were all under a spell during your previous life cycles. This time you don't have that interference. You are all where you were always meant to be. Everything that happens now is a direct result of your actions. That has never been the case before. The previous life cycles don't matter because it was never your actions or your choices. You can't let those insecurities rule your behavior now."

"But it's not just that. You have seen how they all come for her. They think if they have her then they have the power and the control. They want the Origin so why not take the one that has control of it?"

"You are acting out of fear. If we all focused on the 'what ifs' in life, then we would never get anywhere. There are a million what ifs for every situation. You have to focus on what is actually happening and not what could possibly happen. You will drive yourself crazy thinking about all the things that could go wrong."

"Ok, I see your point."

"Good. Now for the most important part of this discussion, I will not tolerate my daughter being treated like that. You will not control her every move and you will not dictate to her what she can and can't do. She is her own person and can make her own decisions. I'm positive she has already told you the same thing. I wanted to let you know I will also be someone that you will not want to deal with if you mistreat her. I have talked to her father, and he knows what he did that was wrong and he feels terrible for it. I know that you were both coming from a place of love and protection but that kind of behavior is harmful and hurtful no matter where it comes from."

Chase is staring down at his hands in shame and mom continues.

"Chase look at me. I love you. You are a son to us. However, I will not sit back and watch you poison your marriage. I'm not saying any of this to make you feel bad but I hope that it helps you to understand that this can't happen again."

Chase has tears in his eyes and he nods his head. Mom squeezes my shoulder on her way out of the room.

Chase turns to me when she has left. "First Landon, then the rest of them, I'm afraid to see who comes in next."

I laugh as he cringes when he hears Rayne. "Oh, they saved the best for last."

He turns to look at her and we can both see the fury in her eyes. She is the most pissed aside from me. Chase sits back in his chair and prepares for her to say what she needs to.

"Of all the stupid, harebrained, idiotic things that you could have done you picked the worst. I don't care if you like what I am going to say or even if you care what I think. I may have started out being one of the most difficult obstacles for you two but this family means everything to me and I will not sit back and watch you be an idiot and treat Annisa like that."

"Rayne, I care what you think. You are family and your opinion always matters. I know what I did was wrong and I deserve all the ass chewing that I have been getting."

"Good, I'm glad you agree that you deserve what you are getting. You have no reason to ever treat any of us like you treated her today. She has never given you any reason to think she can't handle those morons. She has gotten the better of them every time. You are so conceited that you think you are the only one that can protect her. What are all of us, chopped liver? We can help her just as much as you can. You not only insulted her with your behavior but you insulted the rest of us too. Everyone else may be too polite to point it out but you need to know. We are not all just here for our looks. We have just as much power as you and she has more than all of us. Your little two-year-old temper tantrum today was a slap in the face to all of us."

I smirk. Only Rayne can put things in that light. I love her sarcastic take on it and bringing it around to all of them and not all about me but I would never admit it to her.

Chase looks like she has smacked him in the face. "I never meant that none of you could help her. All I was thinking about was that the Faerie King would try and take her away from me."

She snorts. "And when we were all outside, and you were trying to convince us that she needed to come back inside because she wasn't safe outside with us did that mean we could help her?"

He sighs. "I didn't mean it like that."

"I don't care how you meant it. You insisted she needed to be by you so that you could protect her. You didn't trust her to protect herself or any of us to help her. Even when we left with our moms, who are half of the Counsel. You need to get over yourself and deal with the fact that she is not helpless and we are not useless."

She stands and walks out of the room.

Chase looks over at me shell shocked. "I think I just got my ass kicked by a life-sized Barbie."

I laugh when she yells over her shoulder, "And don't you forget it!"

CHAPTER 33

The next couple of days are tense around the house as everyone gets over their anger. Our parents decide to stick around for a few days to make sure there are no problems with the new system with the passageways.

Dad comes to the clearing to check and see how things are going. He is still acting a little weird trying to make sure that I have truly forgiven him for his behavior. He looks around to ensure nobody is there waiting to go through a portal before he asks his questions.

"With not having the contracts and letting them all have free reign to travel where they want and not have to stay on a tour I was a little worried there would be more problems. How is everything going so far?"

I smile. "We haven't had any complaints and I haven't seen anything to indicate that magick is being exposed. I give them a list of the shelters on where they can stay if they want somewhere that is aware that they are magickal. Most of them are using the bed-and-breakfast locations. They find it easier to stay there than trying to get a hotel room."

"Good. I'm glad it all seems to be working out. I haven't seen any requests for prolonged stays or permanent residences come through yet."

"Dad, it's only been a couple of days. You have to give them time to really look around and get a feel for the realm. Now that everyone has free reign in all the realms they are all trying to experience them all to decide where they like the best. I think it will be at least a couple of months before any of those requests come through."

"Yeah, I guess you're right. I was hoping we could get the first of them done and see how the other rulers are truly going to respond to them."

I smile. "The Faerie King has passed a new law stating that any mistreatment of any magickal being is subject to punishment as he deems fit. I thought that left it pretty open for him to not have to punish anyone. Apparently, some of the faeries thought the same thing. I guess one faerie brought his goblin wife and children to meet his faerie family and they were stopped on the way by some faeries that didn't approve. The King has the pathways from the passageways to the town watched and when the guards saw the faeries giving the goblin woman and the children a hard time and taunting them they were immediately brought to the King."

"Really? I wonder what he did."

I smile again. "Apparently, the King summoned the faerie and goblin couple to his castle and they were told to bring the children. When they got there, the faeries that had been harassing them smirked until the King asked the couple to verify that the faeries present were the ones that were harassing them. The couple confirmed it and the King looked to the children and told them they had nothing to worry about because the men that had bothered them would no longer have any magick and would not be able to hurt them."

My dad starts to laugh and I continue.

"The King wants the children to feel safe in his realm so he had them watch as the faeries were stripped of their magick. Word spread fast and there have been no other incidents like that."

"I'm glad to hear the Faerie King is holding up his end of

the agreement. I was a little worried myself he would look the other way when it came to the faeries harassing the other beings. I guess being a father himself he was more aware of the damage things like this could do to children. Since the children are half faerie, he feels he is also responsible for their wellbeing. I'm glad he stepped up and did the right thing."

"The only thing I'm not sure about is how things are going in the troll realm. I have not heard anything yet. I know they have a tendency to be cruel so I'm not sure how many have really ventured into their realm."

Just as I say this King Sebastian steps through the passageway and I look up surprised to see him.

Dad reaches over and shakes his hand. "King Sebastian what a pleasant surprise. We weren't expecting you. Is there a problem?"

He smiles. "Nothing we haven't brought on ourselves, I'm afraid. It seems the other beings are a little scared to visit our realm. Our reputation of being cruel and heartless has been long standing. I must admit it is not an unfair description. I have been working on trying to bring some of the cruelty down a few levels. It has taken a few generations, but each generation gets a little better. My trolls also know that cruelty to any other being is strictly prohibited and will be punished by me personally. Honestly, I never much cared for the cruelty of my people. I have managed to bring it down quite a bit by making the person causing the pain experience the same acts they have inflicted on others. That tends to make them stop and think before they inflict any harm on another. If they don't want it done to them, then they think really hard to see if it is worth the risk of getting caught. I was hoping you could help spread the word of my new law that states the punishment for cruelty to anyone in the troll realm is that they must suffer the same thing."

My dad smiles. "We would be happy to assist you in this. I must admit I myself was a little leery of your trolls due to the cruelty. I could see the enjoyment that some of them got out of inflicting pain on others."

He sighs. "I have now convinced them all that I am serious about the punishment and they all seem to be more relaxed. It seems that the more confidence they have of not being tortured for the smallest little thing the better they all get along. It has really improved the well being of our realm."

"I'm glad to hear that. I will definitely let the other leaders know so they can inform their people. Hopefully, you will begin to get some visitors soon. I know there are quite a few that have wanted to come but have been afraid to do so."

I smile. "I also know of some hybrids that want to know what your realm is like. Unfortunately, their parents have painted a picture that reflects the cruelty and have left a bad taste in their mouths. I will let them know so that they may be willing to bring their children to meet their family and see for themselves how things have changed."

He smiles at me. "I have already talked to the families of the ones you are referring. I have arranged for them to come here and meet up with their lost family members and meet the new ones. I am leaving it up to them if they want to stay here or come back. I can understand the reluctance to bring children that were not raised in our realm there as they would not be prepared to handle what had been common behavior in the past. Now that things are changing they can hear about it first hand from people they trust and can make the decision from there."

"That sounds like the best way to handle that. I'm so glad they are able to meet up with their families. The trolls here were very worried about how their families were faring. They will be very relieved to see they are well and that things are getting better in their home realm."

We talk with the Troll King for a few more minutes and then he goes back to his realm. Dad leaves to talk to the other rulers and let them know what the Troll King had informed us of.

When it is time to close the passageways for the night, I take Chase's hand and lead him through the portal to our beach. It has been tense between us since our fight.

When we step through we walk to the water's edge and look out at the ocean. I stay where I am for a minute and give him a moment to gather his thoughts. I can tell that something has been bothering him ever since our fight and I am hoping by being here he will finally open up to me so we can talk about it.

He sighs. "Do you ever wonder if maybe it wasn't all just the spell we were under? Maybe we don't know how to get it right. Every time it looks like we got it right and things are going well something happens to make it all blow up in our faces."

This is not what I was expecting. "I think that any relationship has hard times they need to work through. We have moved so fast that we really never got a chance to go through all of this at the beginning. We had our connection, and we were so happy that we got it right this time that we rushed everything. We knew we were soul mates, and that we belonged together so we charged ahead at full speed. We didn't take the time to really date. We had so much going on that any alone time we had we used it to talk about what was going on instead of focusing on us."

"Yeah, I guess you're right. I still think we made the right choices now we need to catch up. I wouldn't change finding you and marrying you and sharing my life with you for anything."

I smile. "Good because you are stuck with me now. We need to make sure we make more time for us as a couple. We have been doing a lot better with that since our trip. We have this beach we can escape to and just be in the moment and enjoy being together."

He turns and pulls me close. He wraps his arms around my waist and my body melts into his. He smirks. "Our bodies fit perfectly together. No matter how we come together it is like a puzzle that fits in place."

I smirk. "We were meant to be together, so it only makes sense that our bodies would fit together. I must admit that I rather enjoy the way our bodies come together."

He laughs. "Yeah, the one area we have never had a problem with is the sex. It has always been amazing."

I continue to smirk. "Let's hope that after we have kids you still feel the same way."

He leans back to look at me with panic in his eyes.

I laugh. "Don't look so scared. I meant someday. I'm not ready for kids yet. We still have lot to work on before we are ready to bring a child into this world. We may know each other but we are still learning on how we work as a couple. We have to get a lot better about that before we can even think about kids."

He lets out a relieved sigh. "I was really hoping that wasn't you hinting that you wanted a baby. I am still working on not being so overbearing with you. I couldn't imagine if we had a daughter and I had to work on not being overbearing with both of you."

"Are you saying that if we have a son you won't be that way with him?"

"I hate to admit it but I would probably be worse on him. I would be so intent on making sure he knows everything he needs to know to take care of himself and also help protect you. I would drive him crazy with what I would want him to learn and how fast I would want him to learn it."

"It's a good thing we have plenty of time to get you over those tendencies. I really want you to enjoy our children when we eventually have them and not be focused on what they need to know but letting them have a childhood and enjoying it with them."

"I'm sure you will make sure that is exactly how it will happen."

I smile. "You bet your ass I will."

ABOUT THE AUTHOR

Miranda Shanklin resides in Central Illinois with her husband and their two children. When she is not working at her day job as a paralegal, running her children to practices or supporting them at events she is writing. She has been an avid reader most of her life and has always dreamed of writing her own books someday. Now that her children are reaching their teenage years she is finding the time to sit down and chase her dream.

Miranda can be found on her website www.mirandashanklin.com or Facebook at www.facebook.com/mirandashanklinauthor

Made in the USA
Monee, IL
11 July 2021